THE SAVAGE HILLS

THE SAVAGE HILLS

by

Carl Eddings

Dales Large Print Books
Long Preston, North Yorkshire,
BD23 4ND, England.

British Library Cataloguing in Publication Data.

Eddings, Carl
    The savage hills.

A catalogue record of this book is
available from the British Library

ISBN   1-84262-261-7 pbk

Copyright © 1966, 2002 John Glasby

Originally published in paperback as
The Big Fury by Tex Bradley

Cover illustration © Faba by arrangement with
Norma Editorial S.A.

Published in Large Print 2003 by arrangement with
Robert Hale Ltd.

Dales Large Print is an imprint of Library Magna Books Ltd.

Printed and bound in Great Britain by
T.J. (International) Ltd., Cornwall, PL28 8RW

1

EDGE OF THE BADLANDS

Late in the afternoon, the sky assumed a white look and the sun was a blazing disc that burned men's backs and shoulders, made every breath a labour. This was the bad time for men on the trail, but the five men who rode hard across the glaring alkali ignored the discomfort, staring straight ahead of them as they rode, eyes slitted against the dust and harsh sunglare, jaws set, flannel shirts drenched with perspiration, clinging to their lean, hard bodies.

Sage Venner, riding in the lead could almost smell the gold that lay somewhere ahead of them. The little voice in his brain kept whispering: *Fifty thousand dollars in gold and banknotes. Fifty thousand dollars!* The voice of greed argued that their plan was a surefire success, that if they played their cards right, nothing could go wrong. A deep-seated eagerness took a hold of him. Gold hunger was stronger than food hunger or weariness, stronger than the discomfort from the irritating, scouring grains of sand and caustic dust that swirled about them, kicked up by the pounding hoofs of their mounts.

He and the boys had ridden for miles, with the wind and sun and sand their enemies. This was country they all knew from the old days. Federals had swarmed through it in large groups, companies and battalions of them, but they had never routed the men of the South. Three months before, they had held up a north-bound stage and taken the strongbox off it, containing a little over two thousand dollars in gold and coin. Since then, they had passed wanted notices in almost every small frontier town through which they had ridden. The likenesses had not been good and Venner felt confident that they would never be recognized. But they would have to be careful once they approached Benson. The largest bank in the county was situated here and there had been three attempts to rob it in the past two years, all ending in failure, the would-be robbers lying dead or dying in the wide street. Now it was claimed that nobody would ever rob the bank at Benson and get away with it. Maybe it was this challenge, as much as the knowledge of all that money there, which had fired Venner with the desire to carry out this daring raid.

Sage Venner was a professional killer. In the days of his youth, he had fought with the Confederates against the North, had ridden with Quantrill, and it had been this episode in his life which had coloured his thinking once the war was over. With Quantrill, he had killed for various reasons, few of them to do with the war itself. Pride, greed, often sheer cussedness. Then, a year after Quantrill was caught, a man had offered him two hundred dollars to call a man and shoot him down in a street in Abilene. The skills he had learned so well in his youth had stood him in good stead and he had completed the assignment in a rapid and business-like style.

Then, hounded from Abilene by the law, he had teamed up with the men who now followed him: all fast men with a gun. Ed Borge, Clem Lander, Matt Tollen, scarred of face and twisted of mind, and Verge Monroe, short and thin, with lips which always seemed to be twisted into a perpetual sneer against life.

Dipping downgrade, they rode along the dried-out bed of a winding creek, lowering their heads a little, bending in the saddle so that they could gain the maximum protection from the brushy banks on either side which kept off the wind and driving dust. But the banks closed off all sight of the country through which they rode and Venner had the strangely uneasy feeling that he was riding through a tunnel. Anyhow, he tried to tell himself fiercely, who was there up in this stretching wilderness to see them? It was easy for a man to get the fidgets if he kept imagining that there were unfriendly eyes watching him from every patch of brush and scrub.

They climbed out from the creek bed, reached a rocky knob of ground that thrust up from the flatness. Three stunted oaks grew from the thin soil and that was all. As they approached the spot, Venner threw a quick, appraising glance at the sky. Almost four o'clock, he estimated, judging by the position of the sun. Another five or six hours' journey before they hit Benson. He reckoned they ought to get there somewhere around midnight so as to attract the least amount of attention and that meant there was time to rest their horses here for an hour or so. He signalled to the others to rein up, jerked his own mount to a halt and got down, looping the reins over the animal's head.

'We'll rest up here for an hour,' he said sharply.

Borge moistened his dry, cracked lips and then wiped them with the back of his sleeve. 'We hit Benson about midnight, ain't that the plan, Sage?'

'That's right. And we ride in separate, get rooms in separate saloons and we don't see each other until tomorrow mornin'. You all got that?'

The rest nodded. Getting down, they moved into the sparse shade of the trees. The sun was pressing down on the dry, burned earth about them with a ruthless force and although there was a spring bubbling out of the arid ground near the trees, the water was low and brackish. Monroe tasted it, spat it out after he had swilled it around his mouth.

'Tastes bad,' he said tersely. He unscrewed the top of his canteen, drank thirstily, letting the water slide down his throat. 'Hell, I'll be glad when we hit town. I need whiskey to wash this trail dust out of my throat.'

'You'll get it when we reach Benson,' Venner said. He leaned his back against the trunk of one of the trees, seeking what little shade there was. Even here, the air seemed to have been pulled over a vast inferno before it reached them, striking his lungs with a searing force. He turned things over in his mind, as he had all the way from Coronado Springs, the last town they had passed through on the trail. There had been Pinkerton men in that town, he remembered with a fierce grin. Whether they had been looking for them or not, he had been unable to tell. But they had walked quite openly through the town without attracting any unwelcome attention, had got fresh horses and supplies. There was the feeling in his mind that things were going to go well for them. Sitting there, he could almost feel all of that gold in his hands, running through his fingers.

Once they made a killing like that, they would be able to head for the border, slip into Mexico, maybe down San Antonio way where they would be able to buy all the whiskey and women they wanted. Fifty thousand dollars, even split five ways, would last each man for life.

An hour later, when the sun moved around the side of the tree, continuing its slow drop towards the western horizon, he ordered the men to saddle up once more. They entered a long line of mesquite, ran parallel to the trail for a mile or so and then swung back to it. The wind had picked up force again and now the sun shone more dimly in the dust-filled sky. They reversed their neckpieces, tied them over their noses and mouths, rode with heads lowered in an attempt to reduce the scouring severity of the dust that swirled about them.

Time passed and a reddish tinge touched the sky, turning the whole of the western horizon to a dull flame. Not until it was dark did the men ease the punishing pace of their mounts. The norther that had blown the dust over the trail eased, and then ceased altogether with sundown and the air cleared as if by a miracle. The first of the skysoldiers came out, gleaming faintly in the east; then as the night came sweeping in, more stars appeared until starshine was a shimmering glow all about them, picking out the trail as a lighter streak of dust against the dimness of the surrounding terrain.

Now the open country around them was cut off by rocky upthrusts. Except for an occasional flight of quail, flushed out by their approach, nothing moved. Thirty minutes later, they gave their mounts chance to blow by an overhang in a shallow rock cave. While the others waited, Venner rode his mount to the top of a low rise. He had a soldier's nervous desire to see the ground around him scouted for any sign of trouble and he sat tall and straight in the saddle, pushing his sight through the darkness in all directions without seeing anything. Riding back, he nodded to the others: 'Seems like nobody uses this trail much these days,' he observed.

Tollen had his canteen to his lips. He gave a noisy swallow, then replaced the top. 'You sure all that money will be in the bank at Benson tomorrow, Sage? If it ain't the big place you reckon, could be that your information is wrong.'

'I say that the gold is there,' said Venner quietly, deadly quiet. 'That's all you need to know. You gettin' any ideas about this plan?'

Tollen shrugged, then shook his head slowly, 'Just wanted to be sure,' he muttered defensively. 'I don't like riskin' my neck for nothin'.'

'Have we done that any of the other times?' Venner persisted.

'No, but I–'

'Then keep quiet,' Venner snapped. 'You've all been told the layout. I've got everything organized.'

Tollen worked on the makings of a smoke,

but his eyes never once left the other's face. Lighting the cigarette, he drew the smoke deep into his lungs. 'Just got to thinkin' about those other *hombres* who figured that robbin' this bank was a pushover. Heard they all died in the street without reachin' their horses.' His lips drew back in a grin that showed his teeth as a white gleam in his shadowed face. 'A man gets to thinkin' about such things on the trail.'

'Then forget 'em.' There was a trace of fury in the other's tone as he locked his gaze with Tollen's. 'Those men were fools, bunglin' fools. They rode into town in a bunch, crashed the bank and just about told everybody in Benson what they intended doing. Nobody's goin' to know that we're goin' to rob the place until it's over and finished and we're headed out of town. Just so long as you all do as you're told there won't be any mistake.'

For a moment, a climbing tenseness came to the men clustered there. Hard men who followed a hard, dangerous trade. Men who had to be fast on the draw to stay alive, who were just one jump ahead of the law in more than half a dozen states. In the past, each of them had had their share of brutal, dangerous leaders. But this was different.

Here was a man who could, if he wanted, build up a situation to forcing point. If he had to, if Tollen persisted, then Venner would kill him. Every man knew that. So also did Tollen. He deliberately kept his hand swinging well away from the guns strapped to his waist.

'You want us to follow you blindly into Benson?' he asked pointedly, 'is that it?'

'That's it,' Venner affirmed. His grey eyes swept over Tollen and then on to the rest of the men. 'I can bring off this robbery. I *mean* to bring it off. But to do it, I demand immediate obedience from all of you.'

There was a long, taut silence save for the distant howling wail of a coyote, undulating up and down a weirdly musical scale. Then Borge uttered a harsh laugh. 'I reckon you've led us well in the past, Sage,' he said. 'Tollen didn't mean anythin' by this. Just wanted to be sure, that's all.'

Venner turned abruptly in the saddle, then gave a quick nod. 'Then I'll hear no more talk of the risk we must take. Nobody gets their hands on fifty thousand dollars without takin' a risk. But once we've got it, then we stash it away someplace until the hue and cry has died down. Then we divide it into five equal parts and ride for the border, down to San Antonio.'

Clem Lander jerked up his head. He regarded Venner quietly for a long moment, then asked, 'Why don't we head out for the border right after gettin' the money?' He asked the question casually.

'Because the law will seal up every god-damned trail to the border. We'd be caught before we got halfway there, and with the loot. That's why I'm leadin' this group. Because I use my head, Lander. The tele-graph would send news of the robbery ahead of us no matter how fast we managed to ride. We have to do it my way or not at all. A month and we'll be able to head back for the money, split it equally, and then head our separate ways. What happens to a man after he gets his share of the loot is his own affair.'

There was a note of sarcasm in his voice as he spoke. All of the men knew what he meant by that remark. A man took his ten thousand dollars and headed away from this part of the territory. Whether he reached the border – with the money, and alive, depended on how fast he was with a gun.

Shortly before midnight, they topped a long, sweeping rise and there in front of them lay Benson. Lights showed in the streets from the windows on either side and Venner surveyed it with interest, sitting easy in the saddle. It looked bigger than he remembered it from five or six years back. But most of the towns in this area were growing fast, booming as the cattle men moved in, as the gamblers, saloon owners, hoteliers moved in. When he had known it there was but the one main street running through; a wide street that was a dusty thoroughfare during the long, drought-filled days of the summer, and a river of ankle-deep mud when the rains came. Now there were streets running off in both directions from it, wooden buildings had sprouted up on the outskirts, warehouses, stockyards, with the railhead dark and devoid of lights on the edge of town.

In the darkness, it was impossible to take all of it in, but he knew now that there would be at least fifty thousand dollars in the bank here. Benson was now an important town along this stretch of the frontier; had grown quickly and because of this, needed plenty of money to help it along. The ranchers would lodge their money with the bank here, the saloon keepers and the merchants. He rolled a cigarette, thrust it between his lips, said coolly to the others reined up on either side of him. 'Well, there she is, boys. By this time tomorrow, the bank there will be at least fifty thousand dollars poorer and we'll be that much richer. Now split up and do like we planned. Don't forget that nobody knows the others until we light out of town once the job is done.'

The rest of the men gave brief nods, rode off along the ridge, some circling the town so as to ride in from the other end. When they were gone, Venner sat quite still, smoking his cigarette, eyes lidded, missing nothing that went on in the town that lay spread out below him.

Dropping the butt of the cigarette on to the dusty earth, he waited in silence for another ten minutes, then gigged his mount and rode down the wide trail into Benson. Dust still lay in the street as he remembered it from all those years back and his mount made scarcely any sound as it walked along the street between the silent, empty warehouses that had grown upon this edge of town. He passed the huge yards of a freighting company, freshly painted wood on the archway at the entrance to the yards. There was, he noticed, a yellow light in the office close by but as he neared the building, the light went out, the door opened, and a man stepped out on to the street. He wore a wide-brimmed hat tilted on to the back of his head, a frock coat and red waistcoat, with a watch chain dangling across the front. There was an expensive cigar thrust between his lips and after locking the door, he deposited the key in his pocket, turned, then paused as he saw Venner.

There was a look of curiosity just visible on the other's face and acting on impulse, Venner reined up close to the man, leaned down in the saddle.

'Where's the best hotel in the town?' he asked quietly.

The other stepped to the edge of the boardwalk, pointed a hand along the street. 'There's the Double Diamond about seventy yards along on this side, mister,' he said. 'Two-storeyed building. You can't miss it. You won't get much to drink there, though. Miss Kern who keeps the place don't hold with strong drink.'

'Guess that won't worry me for one night,' Venner opined. He straightened, nodded his thanks, rode along the main street, aware that the other was still watching him, but giving no indication that he was aware of this scrutiny.

The Double Diamond Hotel was a new building. There had been only an empty space there when Venner had known the town. The livery stable was in the same place, however, and he rode slowly towards it, dismounting just outside as a groom emerged from the darkness, took the horse from him.

'Better brush him down,' Venner said. 'It's been a long ride across that alkali and he's sweated most of the day.'

The other nodded, said nothing. Venner watched as he led the horse into the stalls at the back, then sauntered across to the hotel. As he moved over the street, he threw a swift glance along it to the west. A man was angling across from the far side toward one of the saloons from which a swathe of yellow light still spilled out into the street. As the other passed across the light he recognized Matt Tollen. A moment later, the other had passed out of sight into the saloon, the batwing doors swinging shut behind him.

There was a new atmosphere in Benson, different from that which he remembered. It was becoming a big town: and with it there came that feeling of coldness which always seemed to exist in large places. Inwardly, he felt satisfied at this. It meant that not too much notice would be paid to strangers riding into the town. By now, they would be used to men riding in, staying for a few days and then riding on again.

He noticed the sheriff's office some twenty yards down the street from the hotel. Pausing for a moment on the sidewalk, he glanced up and down the street and then went into the hotel. Potted plants stood on either side of the lobby and there was a carpet on the floor. These, he thought, were all signs that Benson was growing up. Maybe one day it would be a city, but that day was somewhere in the future and he did not think overmuch about it. Moreover, he was acutely aware of the task which faced them the next day and he thrust all other thoughts out of his mind.

Going over to the desk, he leaned forward and tapped the sleeping clerk on the shoulder. The other jerked awake with a start, eyes flying open as he stared up at Venner.

'Sorry, mister,' he said awkwardly, getting to his feet, the chair on which he had been sitting, falling back in his haste. 'Didn't think there'd be anybody ridin' in as late as this.' As he spoke, his gaze strayed to the clock on the wall. It said three minutes to midnight.

24

'Met a man outside the freighting office, said this was the best hotel in town, so I came here,' Venner said. 'Hope he wasn't wrong in what he said.'

'No, sir.' The other shook his head vigorously. 'You want a room by the day, week or month?'

Venner let his brows lift a little at the other's question, then said casually: 'I'll take one for the night. I'm here on business and a lot is goin' to depend on how quickly I get it completed. Any trains leave here for back East?'

The other pursed his lips, thought for a moment. 'Well, the railhead is here in Benson, though they mostly ship out the cattle from the surrounding ranches. I understand there's one train a day heading out. But you can get information from the clerk there. His office opens promptly at nine every mornin', exceptin' Sundays.'

He turned the register as he spoke, waited while Venner wrote in it, then swung it back, glanced down at the signature. 'You'll be in Room Thirty, Mr. Corder,' he said, turning and taking one of the keys from the rack behind him. Handing it over, he went on in a low, hushed tone, 'That man you met at the freighting office, reckon that would be

Eb Courtney. He runs the line. Guess he told you that we don't serve liquor here at the hotel. But if you were to want a little drink and fun, there's plenty goin' on at the saloon just along the street and–'

'That will be enough, Charley,' cut in a sharp voice. 'I'm quite sure that our guest knows what he's doing without any help from you.'

'Yes, ma'am.' The clerk picked up his chair, set it upright, then sat down in it, picking up the paper which lay beside him.

Venner turned, saw a tall, regal-looking woman walking towards him from one of the other rooms. Her hair was a pale gold, swirling about her shoulders, and it was impossible to guess her age. She gave him a warm smile. 'Welcome to the Double Diamond Hotel, Mister–'

'Corder, Samuel Corder,' Venner said.

'I'm Virginia Kern. I own this hotel. Naturally if you want to drink, gamble, then there is the saloon that Charley mentioned.'

Venner shook his head. 'Like I said, I have a lot of business to attend to tomorrow and I've had a hard, long day on the trail. If there is something to eat, I'd appreciate it. I realize that it's late and–'

Virginia Kern gave a faint smile. 'We'll

manage something, Mister Corder. If you'll just go through into the dining room, I'm sure we can get you something.'

'Anything will do,' Venner said, going into the room she indicated. The dining room was empty. Most of the tables had been set for the breakfast the next day, but there were two close to the door, one cluttered with supper dishes and the other empty. He seated himself at the latter, waited while a cook brought in a plate of stew, salt and bread, then a cup of steaming coffee and set them down in front of him.

He ate the stew slowly, relishing every mouthful. It was more than he had expected even here. The food was hot, well-cooked, and it stopped the gnawing pangs of hunger in his stomach. With the plate clean, he sat back, rolled himself a smoke, sipping the hot coffee slowly. He had been tired after that long ride over the Badlands, body brittle, like a board that had lain too long in the sun, twisted and warped by the dry heat which sucked all of the moisture in a man's body out through the pores of his skin. Now he felt better. The coffee had acted as a stimulant. There was, however, a strange feeling of restlessness in him which he could not throw off. In spite of the way in which he had spoken to the others, he was only too well aware of the fact that something could go wrong during the robbery the next day. There was always that element of risk whenever a man tempted the fates; some little thing which it was not possible to plan against.

He finished his coffee, stared through the open door of the diner, looking through the blue haze of tobacco smoke. By now, he thought, the other four men would have found themselves a place to stay in Benson. Not until shortly before ten o'clock the next morning, would the five of them come together again.

Venner woke early the next morning, lay for a moment staring up at the ceiling, thinking: *This is it. The day that we've planned for, and waited for. Now it's here and by this time tonight, we'll all be ten thousand dollars richer than we are right now.*

He dressed slowly and carefully, the long coat hiding the heavy Colt at his waist. When he had finished, he would have been mistaken for a prosperous banker or merchant anywhere. Going over to the window, he looked down into the street. There was the hissing of a locomotive getting up steam down by the railhead clearly audible, and a drunk, lying in the shade of the alley across the street, his legs sticking out into the early sunlight that lay over the town, was the only sign of life that Venner could see. He glanced at his watch. It was early yet, not quite six o'clock. Far off, where the hills lifted above the vast, stretching panorama of the rangeland, sunlight was breaking in a rolling wave over the countryside, spreading outward, touching the streets of the town as the sun rose, softening the harsh contours of the buildings which had clearly been erected for efficiency and not beauty of line. Outside the hotel, the street was wide, flanked by the tall wooden buildings on both sides, but in the dead centre there grew a huge cottonwood tree and around the base of it a wooden seat had been erected.

Five minutes later, he was seated on it, watching the street with an apparent unconcern. Over everything, the sun was beginning to beat down with a furious glare that seemed to shimmer and vibrate into a hard whiteness even at this early hour of the day.

There was a movement along the street and a man stepped out of the saloon, stood on the edge of the boardwalk, looking about him in both directions. It was Tollen. His gaze rested for just a fraction of a second on Venner, then swung away and there was no sign of recognition on his features. Hesitating for just a moment longer, he suddenly turned and swung away along the street.

Venner leaned back and closed his eyes, feeling the warmth of the sun on his body although he now sat in the shade of the tall tree.

An hour later, he stirred himself, went in to breakfast. The sun lifted and it looked as if it was going to be another sun-blistering day.

On the other side of town, Ed Borge had slept badly. The bed in the small saloon had been lumpy, giving him little rest and he had woken in a bad temper. Buckling on his gunbelt, he checked that all of the chambers were loaded and then went over to the window and drank his fill of water from the earthenware pitcher in the basin. He had drunk perhaps a little too much previous evening and it was still difficult to quench his raging thirst. Wiping the back of his hand across his mouth, he forced his mind to control his temper. He would have liked more whiskey, but he knew that this was the day when he would have to keep a clear head and he also knew what Venner was like when he was in a rage, as he undoubtedly would be if any of the gang turned up drunk and jeopardized the entire proceedings.

Washing his face and neck, he poured the rest of the ice-cold water over his head, shook it like a dog emerging from a river, towelled himself dry. Glancing out of the window, he stared up and down the street outside. In the distance, where he guessed the bank to be, there was a tall cottonwood growing in the very centre of the street and he could just make out the figure of a man, wearing a black frock coat, seated on the bench around the tree. Even as he watched, the other rose to his feet and walked towards one of the two-storeyed buildings nearby. From that distance, it was virtually impossible for him to be certain who the man was, but it had looked strangely like Sage Venner.

Going down into the small kitchen at the rear of the saloon, he waited while breakfast was brought for him. The cook was a stout man, wearing an apron thick with grease. He wiped his hands on a cloth hanging from his belt and stood a little distance from the table, eyeing Borge with an expectant stare.

'Does it take long for this place to liven up in a mornin'?' Ed asked.

The other gave him a dull, disillusioned stare. 'Another hour or so and there'll be plenty of folk on the street.' He went over and leaned his back and shoulders against the counter. 'You anxious for company?'

'Nope. Just want to deposit some money in the bank and then be on my way again.' He finished the two eggs and bacon, sipped the coffee. 'I suppose this bank is safe? Heard a lot of a bunch of outlaws in Abilene who robbed the bank there, got away with close on five thousand dollars.'

'Don't reckon that'll happen here, mister. We got a real tough lawman in Benson, name of Joel Fergus.'

Borge nodded, drained the coffee cup, sat back in his chair and made himself a smoke. 'You don't say.'

'That's right. Some *hombres* have tried to take the bank here and one or two have attempted to hold up the overland stage, but so far they ain't got away with it.'

'Then I'm sure my money will be safe. Just so long as this lawman is here in town to keep an eye on things.'

'Fergus'll be back in about an hour or so.

He lit off into the hills after a bunch of drink-crazed Indians last night. Feed them critters up with corn beer and they can run riot.'

Borge's eyes widened a shade at that piece of information, but he gave no other sign that it made any impression on him. So the marshal had been out of town all night. He wondered if Venner knew of this and if he had, why they had not met and taken the bank during the night. Then he put that thought out of his head completely. There was something about Sage Venner that he did not rightly understand, something he had noticed over the months they had been together. He reckoned that even if Sage had known the marshal was not around, and presumably most of the deputies too, he would not have made an attempt to rob the bank during the night. That would have been too easy. There would have been no element of challenge to it then. He wanted to put through the plan he had worked on so carefully for so long, do it in broad daylight. This was to be the first time a bank hold-up had been carried out successfully in broad daylight in this territory.

Getting to his feet, Ed laid a couple of coins on the counter, hitched his gunbelt higher about his waist and strolled towards the door. At the entrance, he paused for a moment, threw a quick glance around him, then stepped off into the thick dust of the street, angling across to the other side of the road. Behind him, in the small diner, the cook leaned his elbows on the counter and followed the other's figure until the man was out of sight. There was a lot about that *hombre* which puzzled him, he reflected idly. He didn't seem the sort of man who would have enough money to want to make a deposit in the bank and there had been that strange look on his face when he had mentioned to him that Fergus had been out of town all night after those crazy Indians. Still, it was nothing to do with him, he thought, wiping the top of the counter with a moist rag, and the other had paid on the nose for the bed and the breakfast, which was more than could be said for some of his regular customers. But he'd bear his suspicions in mind and mention them to the marshal when he next met the other.

From the entrance of the livery stables, Lander and Monroe watched Ed Borge as he crossed the street and settled himself down in one of the seats on the boardwalk, tilting his hat over his eyes to shut out the slanting rays of the sun, his legs thrust out straight in front of him. Both men had slept in flea-infested beds in two of the small dwelling houses along one of the side streets in the town. They had been careful not to meet each other either the previous evening when they had found themselves in the same saloon, or that morning when they had made their way out into the town. Now they stood several yards apart, Lander whittling away at a piece of wood with his bowie knife and Monroe, his arms folded across his chest, apparently taking no interest at all in what was going on around him.

It would be Lander's job to collect the horses and have them ready outside the bank for when the others came out with the loot. Everything, as Venner had pointed out, was going to depend on split-second timing and on each man being in the right position at the right time. The slightest slip-up could mean the difference between success and failure, between having ten thousand dollars apiece and finding themselves with a hempen rope around their necks.

Minutes passed slowly. Around them, the town came alive. A bunch of riders rode by, heading out of town, their horses kicking up the smothering, irritating clouds of dust which hung to the still air for long minutes before finally settling. The heat began to make itself felt as the sun climbed higher above the distant range of mountains.

Matt Tollen had moved along the street and was now seated on the low bench around the base of the cottonwood where Venner had been seated almost two hours before. He kept his eyes on the tall bank building some seventy yards away. The doors had opened more than half an hour before and a trickle of people had made their way in and out of the place. Running his fingers along the scar on his face, he tried to keep the climbing tenseness out of his mind. For a moment, he paused while his eyes flicked to the hotel directly ahead of him. There was a movement in the shadowed lobby just inside the door. A moment later, the tall, frock-coated figure of Sage Venner came out, standing for a moment to look in both directions along the street. His probing gaze paused for just a fraction of a second as it rested on Tollen, then moved on as the other nodded his head almost imperceptibly. Tollen drew a deep breath into his lungs. Stiffly, he got to his feet, stifling the tightness in his mind. It was almost time. Inwardly, there was a little sense of worry that he could not rid himself of. All the time he had been in the street, he had seen nobody go in or out of the marshal's office just along the street a piece from the bank, and for some odd reason he could not define, this worried him more than he cared to admit. Whenever they pulled any jobs like this, he always liked to know just exactly where the law happened to be.

Venner moved slowly towards the bank entrance. Tollen stretched himself like a man who had just woken from a doze and moved after him, angling across the street after the other. Out of the corner of his eye, he noticed two men move away from the shadowed boardwalk along the street, recognized Monroe and Ed Borge, all converging on the bank, hands well away from the guns at their hips.

Tollen drew another deep breath into his lungs. A hand dropped down to the heavy belt that hung at his waist. Almost without direction, the fingers loosened the gun in its holster. He ran a dry tongue over equally dry lips, looked for a second behind him. There seemed to be a moment of utter silence in the street. Then, from the direction of the livery stable, there came the slow, rhythmic trend of horses' hoofs. Lander was moving up, leading their mounts behind him.

2

GOLD FEVER

Joel Fergus felt hot and hungry as he rode into the main street of Benson, the rest of the posse strung out behind him. There was, too, a sense of frustration in his mind. They had gone out after that bunch of hooch-crazed Indians but somehow, during the night, they had managed to give them the slip among the foothills of the mountain range and now he was returning empty-handed to town.

Tying his bay to the hitching rail in front of the office, he threw a quick, weary glance along the street, started for the front steps as the rest of the men rode up at his back, then paused for a moment as he spotted the man leading the bunch of horses less than a hundred yards away. As the other moved past him, Joel gave him a piercing glance, then shrugged. The man's face was unknown to him and as there was no sign of trouble anywhere, he brushed the faint tick of suspicion from him and went into the cool shade of the office.

Sharkey, one of the deputies, came in after him, tipping his hat on to the back of his head, wiping his forehead where the sweatband had dug a deep red mark into his flesh.

'Reckon there's nothin' else for us to do now, Marshal,' he said, making it a hopeful question. 'Guess me and the boys can get some rest. It's been a long night, tryin' to run down those critters.'

'Sure, Jeb,' Joel nodded. 'I doubt if they'll be in town for a while even though we lost 'em.'

Sharkey went out, yelled an order to the riders. The men swung their mounts away from the boardwalk, trotted them over to the livery stables. From there, they headed for the saloons and restaurants. Within a minute the street was almost empty.

Joel glanced around the office, at the sheaf of papers on his desk which would have to be attended to, then decided to leave them until he had had a drink, something to eat and a wash. After that, he would take a walk along to the telegraph office and have a word with Jenny Tindel.

Crossing the street, he pushed open the door of the saloon, but there was too much noise, too much blue cigarette and cigar smoke in the air for his liking, and he let the door swing shut again, continuing along the boardwalk until he came to the small restaurant. Cookie Henders glanced up from behind the bar, gave him a quick nod of welcome as the other lowered himself gratefully into a chair at one of the tables.

'Any luck with those goddamned Indians, Marshal?' he asked, pouring out the coffee and bringing it over. Placing it in front of him, he went on: 'I'll get you the usual in five minutes.'

'Thanks, Cookie.' Joel rubbed the muscles at the nape of his neck. 'No, we lost 'em up in the foothills. Too many trails there that a man can take and lose himself among the rocks. Besides, those Indians know how to cover their trails well, drunk or sober.'

Henders nodded. He went back to the door leading into the other room. Joel sat back in his chair, listening to the sounds of the town outside. There was a dull, deep-seated weariness in his body and his eyes and face stung where the caustic dust had formed a mask, caking over his flesh. Five minutes later, Cookie Henders returned with the breakfast.

'Smells good,' Joel observed. 'Just what I

need after last night.' He drank some of the coffee, ignoring the fact that it burned the back of his throat as it went down.

Cookie pulled out the chair opposite him and sat down, his face serious. He waited in silence while Joel had finished the bacon and eggs, then asked: 'More coffee?'

Joel nodded, pushed the cup forward and made a smoke while the other filled it. 'Anything happen while I've been away, Cookie?'

'Depends,' said the other quietly. 'Had a stranger stay here for the night. Rough-lookin' customer. Said he wanted to deposit some money with the bank before ridin' out. Wanted to know if the bank here was safe because he's heard that outlaws had robbed the bank in Abilene and got away with plenty of money. Seems he was all-fired anxious to know whether there was the same chance of that happenin' here.'

'Maybe one of these *hombres* who's made a little money and wants to make sure he don't lose none,' Joel observed, digging into his pocket for a sulphur match. He lit the cigarette, drew the smoke deeply into his lungs, letting it out again through his nostrils. 'Probably doesn't trust banks at all, but he's scared of carryin' money around with him.'

'That could be,' said the other, evidently not entirely convinced.

'You figure there might be somethin' more to it than that?'

'I got that feelin',' affirmed the other. 'Besides, he seemed interested in hearin' that you'd been out of town with a posse all night. Tried not to show it, but I figure I can read what a man's thinkin' by what shows through on his face.'

'So you think he may be here to make trouble.' Joel glanced down at the redly glowing tip of his cigarette. He shook his head faintly, remembering the long hours of the night; dark, cold hours chasing after nothing. He rubbed his eyes where grit had worked its way under the lids making them sore and tender. 'I'll keep my eyes open for this *hombre*, Cookie. But I think you're wrong about him. If he intended makin' any trouble, he'd have done it through the night, not waited for broad daylight.'

Leaving the restaurant, Joel made his way to the telegraph office near the edge of town. Jenny Tindel was sweeping out the small room when he entered. Her features relaxed suddenly as she saw who it was.

'I didn't hear you ride into town, Joel,' she said, smiling a little with relief. 'You must have been gone all night.'

'We were,' he acknowledged. 'We came in from the north.'

'Did you catch those men?'

He leaned on the counter, shook his head. 'They made it into the hills just before dark. We spent most of the night huntin' for them, but they'd covered their trails pretty well. Maybe if we'd had an Indian with us, we might have found them before dawn.'

The door leading to the back of the office opened and Tom Tindel came in. He threw Joel a warm glance. 'Heard from Cookie that you didn't get those men, Joel,' he said. 'Too bad. Still I figure they won't be comin' back into town in a hurry.'

'Cookie mentioned to me that he had a stranger put up at his place last night, Tom. Any other men arrive while I was away?'

'Ain't heard of any, Joel. You think there might be trouble?'

'I'm not sure. If there was just this one *hombre*, I doubt it. But that gang of outlaws who hit Abilene a few weeks ago were reported as headin' in this direction.'

'But weren't there five or six men in that bunch?' queried the other.

Joel hesitated, then nodded. 'That's right. Guess I'm just too tired to think straight right now.' He rubbed his chin, eased his aching shoulder blades against the counter.

Then a gun roared somewhere along the street – three sharp and distinct shots. The swiftly-dying echoes were still ringing in the stillness as Joel launched himself across the office towards the door, right hand streaking down for the gun at his waist.

Ten minutes before, Sage Venner pushed open the door of the bank and stepped inside. He knew, without turning his head to see, that the other three men were moving forward close on his heels, apparently unconnected with each other, merely three more customers. It was a large bank, larger even than the one in Abilene. There were two tellers at the windows and in a smaller enclosure off to one side, a man sat with his jacket off, engaged in muted conversation with a tall, red-faced man. There were five customers in the bank apart from this man and Venner's keen-eyed gaze also took in the man beyond the tellers' windows, standing close to the vaults.

Walking forward slowly, keeping his eyes on the men in front of him, Venner moved towards the shirt-sleeved man, paused as he drew level with the enclosure. He noticed, out of the corner of his eye, Tollen and Borge move over to the two windows, standing in line behind the other customers. Verge Monroe had taken up his allotted position near the door, lounging against the wall, thumbs thrust inside his gunbelt, a cigarette dangling unlit from his lips.

A moment of stillness and then Tollen and Borge lifted their hands and there were Colts pointing menacingly at the tellers behind the windows. Tollen said in a loud voice that carried to every corner of the bank: 'All right, folks! This is a hold-up. Everybody do as they're told and nobody will get hurt!'

The two tellers stared through the iron grilles at the men, lifted their hands slowly. Venner saw the shirt-sleeved man, hidden by the bulk of the beefy-faced customer, move his hand slowly towards the stock of a shotgun which protruded from the counter less than a foot from him. His fingers were closing over it when Venner said softly, menacingly: 'I wouldn't do that if I were you, friend.'

The man jerked up his head, eyes widening in stunned surprise as he stared down the barrel of the Colt levelled on him. Hurriedly, he withdrew his hand, sat straight behind the desk. The other man, running his tongue over his lips in a nervous fashion, placed his hands quickly on top of the desk and kept them there.

Venner smiled grimly at the fear which showed on the shirt-sleeved man's face. He had been the unknown quantity always present in things such as this, something to be guarded against. When he had stepped into the bank, he had placed this man as a dangerous element. Swinging slightly to the right, he moved the Colt to cover the customers. One of them, a well-dressed woman, promptly fainted and lay in a huddled heap on the floor less than three feet from Ed Borge. A man, standing a few feet away moved towards her, then halted in mid-stride as Tollen said sharply. 'Leave her be! You'll be able to tend to her when we've gone.' Swinging back to the tellers, he ordered: 'Open up the grilles and start shovin' the money into these bags.' He tossed a couple of empty wheat sacks through the teller's windows. 'And hurry! Do as you're told and you'll be all right. One wrong move, and you're both dead.'

Venner watched out of the corner of his eye, keeping most of his attention concentrated on the two men in front of him, still wary, guessing that the bank attendant might go for the scatter-gun if he thought there was a chance of pulling off such a move. The other man, standing close to the vaults, had his hands lifted high over his head, his fearful gaze fixed on the three men who covered the employees with their guns. He evidently had no illusions as to what would happen if he made a move towards the gun which lay on a table some three feet from where he stood.

The two tellers were busy thrusting gold and dollar bills into the sacks under the watchful eyes of Tollen and Borge. At the door, Monroe glanced along the street every few seconds. The tellers finished their task, handed the sacks back to Tollen and Borge.

'What's it like?' Venner called, not taking his eyes off the men in front of him.

'Not much,' Borge called back. He vaulted over the counter, moved past the two terror-stricken tellers and went to the vaults. 'All right,' he said tautly to the man standing there. 'Where do you keep the gold?'

The other shook his head. 'That's all we keep here,' he said, his voice quavering a little. 'Most of the gold went out on the stage two days ago and–'

'You're lyin',' snapped Borge. He jammed

the barrel of the Colt hard into the other's midriff, just above the belt. The man bleated with agony and backed away a couple of paces until he came up against the vault, where he stood, shaking a little, his features a ghastly, frightened mask. 'Now get the gold out of those vaults and put it in the sacks.' He waved the Colt threateningly.

The bank employee swallowed thickly, then took the sacks from Borge, moved aside and swung open the heavy metal door of the vault. Borge stood over him while he filled the sacks.

Still no sound from the street outside. With an effort, Sage Venner forced himself to relax. Everything seemed to be going smoothly, just as he had planned. But whatever happened, they had to hurry, not become too complacent. At any moment, somebody might happen along and give the alarm before Monroe could silence him. Once a single shot was fired, the entire town would be alarmed and then they would have a minute perhaps, certainly not much longer, to make their getaway. He sucked in a sharp breath, felt sweat break out on his forehead, beginning to trickle down into his eyes. But the gun, lined up on the men in front of him, never wavered, his finger bar-straight on the trigger. He saw the man in shirt sleeves swivel his eyes a moment later at a sudden movement at the door of the bank.

Not turning his head as he heard the sound, Venner said: 'Everythin' all right back there, Monroe?'

'Just another customer come to join the fun.' There was a trace of amusement in the other's voice and Venner knew he had everything well under control.

Near the vaults, Borge hissed: 'Hurry up with that gold. We don't have all day to waste.'

Finally, both sacks were filled. Borge called: 'Cover me, Matt.' Thrusting his Colt into leather, he picked up the two sacks as if they weighed nothing, carried them back to the counter, heaved them over on to the floor and clambered after them. Stooping, he picked them up once more, said sharply: 'That's it, I reckon, Sage.'

Venner nodded. 'Right, then let's get out of here.' He backed away towards the door, covering everyone as the rest of the men moved out. Pausing at the entrance, he said menacingly: 'Anybody try to be a hero and follow us and he'll wind up with a bullet for his pains.'

Swinging, he ran down the boardwalk to where Lander sat waiting with the horses. Borge had already fastened the heavy sacks to his saddle and was climbing up. As yet, there had been no alarm given from inside the bank and the few townsfolk in the street gave them only a cursory glance.

They had wheeled their mounts away from the boardwalk, were heading along the street when the beefy-faced individual who had been engaged in conversation with the shirt-sleeved man appeared in the doorway, a pistol in his fist. Exposing himself recklessly, he loosed off three shots in quick succession. Crouching low in the saddle, Venner kicked his heels against his mount's flanks, urging it on along the street. There were no more shots coming after them as they rode headlong down the dusty street, but a confused shouting rose at their backs and ahead of them, where the telegraph office stood a little distance from the rest of the wooden shacks at this end of town, Venner saw the man step out of the doorway, lifting his gun to cover them. He caught the flash of sunlight on the badge the man wore on his shirt as he lifted his arm.

He jerked his own Colt from its holster, loosed off a snap shot at the other, saw the slug go wide, tearing a sliver of wood from the doorpost. The marshal ducked, then fired several shots in quick succession as they thundered past him and out of town. Clinging to the reins, bending as low as he could, Venner heard the dull hum of lead passing over his shoulders. Then he was past the other and in that same second, saw Monroe jerk in his saddle, almost lose his hold on the reins, swaying as the slug tore into his shoulder. There was blood on the front of his shirt as he struggled to remain in the saddle, his features ashen.

Urging his own horse forward, Venner drew level with the other, reached over and gripped him tightly by the arm, his mount matching speed with Monroe's automatically.

'Think you can make it, Verge?' he called loudly.

Monroe's teeth were gritted tightly together as a spasm of pain lanced through his body. Slowly, he nodded his head, the muscle of his jaw lumping under his skin. 'I can ... make it,' he got out.

'Good. We'll head for the hills. When we get there we'll find a place to hide up and stash the money until it's safe to pull out for the border. Stick with it, Verge.'

He saw the other nod again, grip the reins with both hands although the effort to do so cost him dear, sweat streaking his forehead, dripping from his eyebrows. They were now well clear of the town, heading out through rocky, rugged country towards the range of hills in the distance. They looked a long way off and Venner had no delusions about what was happening in Benson at that very moment. The marshal would be getting his posse together and would follow their trail in ten or fifteen minutes at the latest.

Venner felt certain that if they could maintain this fifteen minute lead over the posse until they reached the foothills, their chances of getting clear were good. They knew this country from the old days, something which that lawman would not know. Their horses were fresh and were being pushed to the limit now. In places, they left the main trail, cut across the flat, featureless country, choosing the hardest ground they could find to leave few tracks.

The valley stretched ahead of them for an interminable distance, clear to the hills, the sunlight pouring down on it in dizzying waves that hurt the eyes and made everything shimmer and shake as though they were looking at it through a depth of water.

Venner blinked his eyes as the sweat ran into them, knowing that the heat head had not yet reached its piled-up intensity.

He selected a wide, deep ravine that opened up ahead of them half a mile further on, put his mount into it, motioning the others to follow. The ravine stretched for a mile or so through the rough country and he guessed that so long as they were riding along the bottom of it they would be out of sight of any pursuers. Threading their way along the descending bed of the steep-walled ravine, around gigantic boulders which thrust themselves up from the ground, at times almost filling the entire passage so that they were forced to slow and squeeze their way past them, legs scraping against the rough walls, they made their way through occasional narrow-walled fissures in the rocks, over high ridges which seemed virtually unscalable, and by the time they emerged, he had the feeling that by striving to throw the posse off their trail, they had lost valuable minutes. He swung in the saddle as they came out into the open once more and glanced quickly behind him. Their dust lay in a grey-white screen behind them, hanging motionless in the still air. Then, far behind them, a cloud of dust no bigger than a man's hand showed on the horizon, marking the position of the posse from Benson. He nodded grimly. Inwardly, he reckoned that the others were about five or six miles distant, near enough, yet they clearly had not gained much in spite of the fact that they had moved off the trail.

Switching his gaze to Monroe, he said tightly: 'How's that shoulder of yours now, Verge?'

'Feels like a red-hot iron inside my shoulder, bein' twisted round and round,' he said thickly. He reached down for his canteen, lifted it to his lips and tried to drink, but his hand was shaking so badly that most of the water spilled down his face and dribbled from his chin.

'Better go steady with that water,' Tollen advised. 'We've still got fifteen or twenty miles of desert to cross before we reach the hills and there ain't no waterholes there at this time of year. Everythin' is all dried up.'

Venner gave a quick nod of agreement. He pointed to the distant riders. 'There's the posse boys. They'll stick with us until we reach the hills. Once we get there, I figure we can give 'em the slip. You reckon you can hold out until we get there, Verge.'

'Sure.' Monroe grinned weakly. 'You ain't

goin' to get rid of me that easily. I intend to be around when that gold is shared out.'

Venner said nothing more, but pulled hard on the reins, kicked his horse's flanks, dragging rowels over the flesh. The others came after him, Monroe swaying from side to side in the saddle, face twisted into a grimace of pain as every movement brought agony into his body, lacing with fiery fingers through his muscles. He blinked his eyes against the glaring sunlight, felt the heat lay a searing finger on him. The hills which were their destination seemed as far off now as they had almost two hours before when they had first ridden out of Benson. He tried to fix his gaze on the heavy sacks which swung from the sides of Tollen's saddle and the heavier ones containing the gold which Borge was carrying. He knew that it was only fixing his mind on these that he would be able to summon up the strength and endurance to carry him to the hills. He recalled what Venner had said the previous night when they had reined up before heading into Benson. The money and gold would be shared five ways, but it would then be up to the individual to keep his share. He knew that in the mind of every other man in the bunch, there was the thought that maybe he wasn't going to make it, that it would only have to be shared four ways.

The posse rode north-west out of Benson, with Joel Fergus showing the way. His saddle was a fresh mount taken from the stables, but most of the horses his deputies were riding were those they had used during the night, tired horses which could not possibly match the speed of the mounts which the outlaws had. He shaded his eyes against the sunlight at regular intervals, searching for any sign of their quarry. Topping a low rise less than two miles back, he had spotted their dust, noticed that they had been riding the floor of Swallow Canyon which explained why they hadn't been seen earlier. He guessed from that, that at least one of these men knew this part of the territory well.

For the most part, they rode in silence, each man engrossed in his own thoughts. The raid on the bank had been well planned and well executed. If Bert Hackett, the grain merchant, hadn't taken things into his own hands, defied the bandits and fired those warning shots, the chances were that the outlaws would have gained a better lead. As it was, he estimated that they were about twenty minutes ahead of the posse, probably drawing further away all the time on their fresher horses.

The trail became rougher as they progressed and overhead, the sun lifted inexorably to its zenith and he told himself that none of the men riding with him had had any sleep for almost two days. From what had happened the previous night, he knew with a sick certainty that once these men hit the hills, they would stand a good chance of losing themselves among the multitude of trails through the low foothills and it would be like looking for the proverbial needle in a haystack trying to find them.

They had lost those Indians after chasing them across this stretch of dry, arid wilderness; the same thing would possibly happen with these *hombres*. He clenched his teeth in his head so tightly that the muscles of his jaw hurt with the strain he was exerting and he forced himself to relax. Goddamnit, he thought tautly, he wouldn't let these men escape. Nobody had robbed the bank in Benson and got away with it. This was a case far different from those drunken Indians who had merely loosed off a few rifle shots, disturbing the peace, and doing little real damage. He had felt only a vague disappointment at losing their trail. He couldn't count the number of times drunks had let off steam in town in that way.

Beside him, Jeb Sharkey sat with his hands holding the reins lightly, his hat brim pulled well down over his eyes. He might have been asleep in the saddle for all the interest he seemed to show in what went on around him, and the loose, easy way in which his body swung to every motion of his mount. But Joel knew that the other was far from asleep and he missed nothing.

Swinging around the tall bluffs that lifted themselves in awesome majesty out of the desert, they caught a glimpse of the outlaws again, spurring their mounts on at a punishing pace. Pity they hadn't caught just one of those Indians, Joel mused; eyeing the small dust cloud. It might have been possible to drop any charge against him if he would have agreed to track down these men once they reached the hills. Very little missed an Indian's sharp eyes. This was what they were born for, trailing a man through the brush. He would have given nothing for their chances if he had an Indian with him.

Noon came and went in a tremendous

pressure of light and heat that brought the moisture in their bodies rushing to the surface, oozing from every pore. In the middle of the afternoon, they were forced to rest the horses. They had not gained a single yard on their quarry during the whole of the chase, and it had become increasingly obvious that they could not hope to catch them before they reached the comparative sanctuary of the hills.

Sharkey squatted on his haunches on the edge of a low ridge looking out over the plain. There was a worried look on his face as Joel walked over and stood beside him.

'Reckon that we got us a problem, Marshal,' he said. 'They're too far ahead for us to catch before nightfall and by that time they'll be inside the hills. We're goin' to lose 'em for sure like we did those goddamned Indians.'

'I know.' Joel was lighting a cigarette, but he held it and let the match burn out in his fingers.

'Did you recognize any of those *hombres*, Marshal?' asked Cornell, tall and bull-necked. He hitched his pants up a little, stood rubbing his fingers together.

Joel shook his head. 'Never set eyes on any of them in my life,' he admitted. 'I reckon it

60

could be that bunch that hit the bank in Abilene a while back though.'

'Why'd you think that?' asked Sharkey, looking up.

'I was talkin' to Cookie Henders early this mornin' just after we rode in. He said there was a stranger who'd been stayin' there overnight, some fella who happened to mention the outlaws who stuck up the Abilene bank.'

'Then you reckon he was one of that bunch?'

'It figures.' Joel lit his cigarette, dragged the smoke down into his lungs and stared off through narrowed eyes to where the distant riders were cutting across the mesa in the direction of the hills. They're too goddamned far, he thought dully.

They rested for another five minutes and then Joel tossed the butt of the cigarette into the dust, ground it in with his heel and stepped towards his horse. Reluctantly, the rest of the men saddled up, grumbling a little. They had a right to grumble, Joel thought as he led the way down the treacherous slope on to the mesa. A long night out after drunken Indians with nothing to show for it but aching bodies and tired limbs; and then out again in the blistering heat of the day, chasing after a bunch of outlaws who would probably get away too.

Funny though that they hadn't headed due south for the border. Could be that they had thought ahead and guessed that he would have sent that message to the sheriffs in the neighbourhood, asking them to watch out for the bunch. Once again, it showed him how well they had planned this whole operation. It pointed undeniably to the leader being a man of intelligence, possessing a cunning and scheming mind.

Inwardly, he was angry because he hadn't foreseen the possibility of this happening when both Cookie Henders and Jenny's father had mentioned the stranger in town. If he'd been a lawman worth his salt, he'd have checked on this at once. It was his duty to check on strangers who rode into town. But now there was not time to go on thinking about what he should have done. The time now was for action. And somehow, he had to try to put himself into the mind of the man who had planned this daring daylight robbery, try to guess what his next move would be.

Certainly those men knew that a posse would be on their trail soon after they had lit out of town. That was inevitable. They had also guessed that a warning would be sent by telegraph to the sheriffs and marshals in a dozen towns along the escape route to the border, a route which nine out of ten outlaws would have taken, trusting to fresh horses to carry them there ahead of any pursuit.

His guess was that these men intended to stash their loot away somewhere in the hills, leave it there until the hue and cry died down, until they had a chance to ride out for the border. Maybe they would also share it out before riding out, then split up, each man with his share, hoping to split any pursuit that way. He smiled grimly to himself as he stared off into the distance. Even among thieves, there would be no sense of honour once that money had been divided out. He could imagine what would happen. Each man would scheme how to grab off more for himself. If that happened, it might at least make his own personal task a little easier. For he had already decided that he would follow these men clear to the Mexican border and beyond to get back that stolen money.

By the time the sun had sunk below the horizon, leaving only a fading splash of flame across the western heavens to indicate where it had been, they were moving into the rising ground that led up into the foothills. Here there were isolated bushes of mesquite and thorn; low, stunted trees that stood as silent sentinels, giving an indication of the thick timber that lay ahead, less than a mile away. There was still the smell of dust hanging in the air, dust lifted by the passage of horses' hoofs.

'They cut in somewhere close by,' Sharkey observed. He moved his horse off to one side, bending low in the saddle, his keen eyes scanning the ground among the low bushes. Finally, he found what he was looking for, gave a shout.

Joel rode over, stared down at the churned up ground where a bunch of men had ridden through. He nodded, his mouth a tight line. 'No doubt about it. This is where they came.' He lifted his head, looked up into the timber that grew thickly a quarter of a mile from them among the lowermost ridges.

'Could be they're headed for the summit, over the other side,' he opined.

Sharkey shook his head in disagreement. 'That ain't likely. They know this country. They'll break off the main trail somewhere. They're in a hurry to get under cover and give us the slip. They'll take the shortest way.'

'It'll be completely dark in half an hour,' observed one of the men. 'We won't be able to follow them then. I suggest we make camp here for the night, go on in the mornin'. If they're not headed for the summit, they'll still be here then. If we go on now we're just as likely to overrun their trail, smear up their tracks in the dark.'

Joel felt dissatisfied, impatient to be on. But he could see the sense in what the other said. With an effort, he forced the feeling of impatience away, still unwilling to let his hopes of an early capture fade into nothing. The desire to ride on after the outlaws rode strongly within him, was difficult to fight down. Finally, however, he said: 'All right. We'll camp up there near the creek. But I want a couple of you men to move off about a hundred yards into the brush, close to the timber, make sure that nobody slips down from there during the night.'

Hackett pulled his horse around, motioned to Collins. The two men rode off into the brush, vanishing into the timber. When they got to an open stretch of ground just inside the first-growth pine, they halted and made cold camp.

Wind scoured down the hillside as the five men turned a sharp bend in the narrow trail they had been following for almost an hour, its coldness beginning to reach them. Venner felt the sweat congeal on his face and along the back of his shoulders. Hunger rolled, growling, in his belly and he felt tired and sore. A quarter of a mile further on, they splashed across a fast-flowing creek, reached an opening in the thickly tangled brush on the far side and halted their mounts, slipping from the saddle as Venner motioned them down.

They had been riding most of the way through thick timber, with the branches meeting overhead to form an almost solid arch of green and consequently it had been difficult to judge the passage of time. Now that they were in the open, it was possible to see that the sky had darkened swiftly, that the first of the stars were visible among the swaying branches of the tall trees and checking his watch, Venner saw that it was a little after ten o'clock.

Walking to the edge of the clearing, close by the stream, he listened for the new sounds of the night that lifted and fell, often barely audible above the bubbling rush of the water, and then lifting above it. Somewhere, horses were moving along the trail down below and he swung his head a little, trying to push his vision through the darkness and the clinging vegetation. But he could see nothing and he knew that the sounds were merely echoes carried by the water, sounds that broke frequently into scattered fragments. Presently they died and he guessed that the riders had paused, were possibly making camp somewhere on the lower slopes.

Tollen hobbled his mount on the edge of the clearing. Harshly, he said: 'You reckon they'll follow our trail up here, Sage?'

'They've stopped at the bottom of the slope. My guess is that they'll wait until mornin' and then try to follow the tracks.'

'And by then, we'll be deeper into the hills.'

'That's right. We'll move out just before it gets light. I've got a little place in mind where we can stash the gold and where it won't be found. Then we lie low for a while until the heat dies down.'

'You figurin' on doin' anythin' for this shoulder of mine?' muttered Monroe. He sat on the edge of the clearing with his back against the trunk of one of the trees. His face was a pale grey blur in the darkness, his hand clutching at his smashed shoulder, where the bullet had torn away muscle and flesh, and the lead was still embedded somewhere near the bone. The blood had long since congealed, absorbing the itching, irritating dust while they had ridden across the mesa through the long afternoon and evening. Now it was a sticky mess as Venner tore the blood-soaked shirt from the wound, peering close at the torn shoulder. A shudder went through Monroe as he probed around with fingers that were none too gentle.

'The slug is still there, ain't it?' muttered the other through his tightly-clenched teeth. 'It didn't come out.'

'It didn't come out,' Venner repeated soberly. 'I'll have to dig for it.' He motioned to Lander. 'Get water from the creek back there. We can't afford to risk lightin' a fire. I'll have to wash it and then we'll hope that infection doesn't start.'

Monroe said nothing, but stared up at him out of narrowed eyes, tongue touching his dry lips. Then his eyes swivelled to one side as Lander stepped out of the trees, carrying his brimming canteen. He handed it to Venner without a word. After washing the blade of his knife, he tore a strip off the other's shirt, dipping it into the ice-cold water and washed the dried blood off the other's shoulder. A fresh shudder went through Monroe and he let his breath go in a thin hiss through his stretched lips. A choking gasp came from him as Venner continued. The wound looked bad and it began to bleed again as he wiped it clean. It was not going to be easy to take that piece of lead out of this torn flesh, but it had to be done. They could not afford to send one of their number into town for a doctor, even if they could get one to ride out into the hills to take a look at Monroe.

'This is goin' to hurt, Verge.' It was simply said, but to Monroe, each word carried the promise of more pain. There was fresh blood on his chest now, trickling from the wound, a stain that spread wetly over his heaving body. He drew in a deep breath that throbbed as it distended the gaping hole in his shoulder. Turning his head, Venner picked up the knife, shook the drops of water from the long blade, held it tightly in his fist as he bent over the other.

Verge Monroe's eyes were very wide, seeming fixed hypnotically on the blade of the knife as it descended slowly. Venner touched his lips with a dry tongue as he steadied himself. The task was not going to be easy, working as he would have to in the dimness. Most of the time he would be working by the sense of touch alone. Like every man who rode the trail, he had learned his own simple form of doctoring. A man never got very far without it. He knew how to set a broken limb and how to find and dig a slug out of an arm or shoulder. But this was the first time he had been forced to do it under these conditions.

He heard a groan escape from Monroe's lips, saw another form, to be held back with a tremendous effort as the man clenched his fists by his sides and drew his lips back from his teeth.

'Think you can get the slug out?' asked Tollen harshly.

'I can do it all right.' Venner's tone was sharper, pitched a little higher than he intended, touched with an edge of climbing tension. 'Hold his arms and legs for me. I don't want him twistin' and squirmin' about while I'm diggin' for it.'

He waited again, waited while the others obeyed, then eased the sharp tip of the knife blade into the wound. Monroe sucked air down into his lungs. His head lifted stiffly from the ground for a moment, hung there, then fell back limply: Tollen said quietly: 'He's fainted, Sage.'

'Maybe it's better that way. He won't feel anythin' now.' Venner dug deeper with the knife, feeling for the metal which he knew to be there. If it had merely lodged against the bone without splintering it, his task would be all the easier. If not, the chances were the other might regain consciousness before it was out.

3

THE SAVAGE HILLS

Ed Borge crouched against the stump of a long-dead cedar, his rifle cocked and lying across his knees, his pale-blue eyes restless as he watched the darkness which lay around the edge of the clearing. The others were asleep, wrapped in their blankets and only occasionally was there a muttering, mumbling moan from Monroe where he lay a few yards away, twisting at times under his blanket as pain bit deeply into his body. Borge felt edgy, tensed. There were sounds off in the night which he could not identify and which he therefore did not like. This country to the north of Benson was reputedly clear of renegade Indians, but he had heard talk in the town of a bunch of them who had been run out of the place by the marshal and who had apparently headed up here into the hills and more than once his scalp had crawled as he had imagined a dark shape behind the thick bushes a few yards from him and his fingers had tightened convulsively on the rifle, swinging it to cover the undergrowth.

His hard-boned length lifted as he got stealthily to his feet, moved over to the point where the narrow trail entered the clearing. He felt sure that they had thrown the lawmen off their trail the previous evening and they would not risk coming along the trail during the night for fear of being ambushed. But with a man such as this marshal was reputed to be, there was no written guarantee that he wouldn't send some men scouting ahead, hoping to take them by surprise.

Reaching the end of the trail, he paused and scanned the battalion of creeping shadows that lay over the broken rocks of the ridge. There were tricky overtones along the trail that endowed every tree and bush with human form and lifted the small hairs on the back of his neck, ruffling them uncomfortably.

Straining every sense to see and listen, Borge tried to separate fact from fancy, knowing how easy it was for the night to play tricks with a man's imagination. After dark, this land came alive and turned on everyone in it. When he was reasonably certain there was no one there, he stepped back into the darker shadows of the trees. If they had to stick around these hills for long before Venner decided it was safe to divide up the gold and head out for the Mexican border, taut, frazzled nerves were going to get the better of them all, he thought tiredly.

After a time, he edged back into the clearing. He glanced at the men lying in the middle of the clearing, saw that one of them was no longer there. A moment later, Venner stepped out of the brush on the opposite side of the clearing, his Colt in his hand. He said in a low, gritty tone: 'Where the hell have you been, Ed?'

'Thought I heard something along the trail apiece,' muttered the other. 'Reckon I must have been mistaken. Nothin' there.'

'You're sure?'

'Positive,' Borge nodded. He lowered his Winchester to his side, leaned his back against a tree, rolled himself a smoke. His nerves were tight like cords within him, but he tried not to show it.

'Could be that those lawmen have decided to move up while it's still dark,' mused Sage Venner quietly. He thrust the Colt back into his holster.

'I don't think so. If there is anybody there,

more likely it's Indians.'

Venner stared at him. 'Indians!' He spoke sharply. 'Why should there be Indians in these hills?'

'Evidently you didn't have your ears open in Benson,' said Borge. 'That marshal and his posse were out all night before last chasin' Indians up here in the hills. My guess is they may still be around, watchin' us all the time.'

Venner said mockingly: 'If there are renegade Indians up here, they'll be too busy keepin' out of the way of the law to bother about us.' He pulled the watch from his waistcoat pocket, glanced at it. 'Another two hours to dawn,' he said. 'You can get some sleep now if you like. I'll keep an eye on things.'

'Reckon there won't be any sleep for me tonight.' Borge jerked a thumb in the direction of Monroe. 'Not with him mutterin' and moanin' through his sleep. Can't we shut him up?'

Venner walked over to where Monroe lay, pulled aside the blanket and stared down at the bandaged shoulder. 'Could be that it's infected,' he said at length. 'If it is then there's nothin' we can do for him.'

'He'll be yellin' for a doctor to be brought

out to him from town as soon as he comes round.'

'Then he'll just have to yell. Because we ain't goin' to risk our necks ridin' back into town just to help him. If he dies, then we share the money four ways. That was what I said before we rode into Benson.'

'Yeah, I remember.' Borge gave a faint nod. 'Could be that you've also got the idea of makin' sure none of the rest of us lives to get to the Mexico border.'

Venner watched him closely, his hand swinging ominously near the butt of the gun at his waist. Then he gave a sharp laugh, relaxed and said: 'You get the craziest ideas at times, Ed.'

'Maybe. But I figure I'll be keepin' a close watch on my share of the money when I get it. Just how long do you figure on keepin' us up here in these goddamned hills once we've stashed it away?'

'I'll decide that,' Venner snapped. He paused as Monroe uttered a faint moan, then twisted on to his good side. For a moment it was as if he had regained consciousness, then he lapsed into unconsciousness again, lay still. 'I planned this raid and it went through without much trouble. I still give the orders around here. Remember if you're caught by

76

those lawmen, it'll be your neck in a noose.'

'All right,' Borge grumbled. 'So you planned it fine. But don't expect the rest of us to rot here with all that money lyin' around. We may start gettin' ideas.'

'What sort of ideas?' asked Venner tightly.

'We'll see,' countered the other. 'Just don't try to push us around too far even though you are the leader now.'

Venner half listened to the other's voice. He knew better than to push the issue with Borge right now. There would undoubtedly be a better opportunity for that some time in the future. Borge was a simple-minded man, relying on his brute strength to see him through. A useful man, fast with a gun, but unable to think things out for himself and foresee the logical conclusions of any actions he might make.

Abruptly, he jerked his head around. An alien sound reached him out of the night stillness. Borge had also heard the sound, for his left hand reached out and grasped Venner's upper arm, fingers tightening with a steel-like grip.

'Stay here,' Venner whispered softly. 'I'll go take a look. I don't want to shoot unless I have to. That would warn those lawmen down the slope.'

He slipped silently across the clearing, moved quickly to his left to where the trail joined the open space, flinched momentarily at the first cold bite of the wind sighing along the trail, funnelled by the trees on either side which formed an almost impenetrable barrier. He slid for a few yards along the trail, keeping his head low, his Colt out, fingers on the trigger. Then he paused to listen for a repetition of the sound which had disturbed the stillness.

If Fergus had placed the trail under surveillance, where would the watching man place himself? he wondered, searching the shadows with his gaze. He would certainly want to be able to watch both sides of the ridge so that they could spot the gang if they moved out into the open before dawn. Very likely, he reflected, the sentry would be up there among the pines which grew out of a vast outcrop of rock some twenty yards away.

Bending, Venner crept through the trees, circling the point where he figured the posseman would be, came to much thicker growth at the side of the trail and here was forced to move more slowly. Ten minutes later, he reached an open crop of bare ground, lifted his head very carefully and peered down. For a long moment, he lay on his stomach, hand holding the gun thrust out in front of him, eyes narrowed. Nothing moved in the long shadows down below him. Had he been mistaken? Perhaps there was no one there – or the other was crouched down somewhere else.

A faint sound in the brush off to his right made him whip round, bringing the Colt to bear. But the shape he spotted was almost fifty yards away, moving rapidly up the slope. For a moment, he was tempted to loose off a shot in spite of his earlier decision, then lowered the gun. He had only been able to catch a brief, fleeting glimpse of the man as he moved across a patch of open ground, but what he had seen had been enough to tell him it had not been a white man. That had been an Indian, most likely one of those chased up here by the posse.

After making certain there were no more in the vicinity, he went back to the clearing. Lander and Tollen were awake, seated cross-legged with their blankets held about them. They eyed him curiously as he entered the clearing.

'Goddamned Indian,' he said angrily. 'Must've been hidin' up there on the ledge watchin' us. No idea how long he'd been there or what the devil he thought he was doin'.'

'Think he could've been sent up by those lawmen?' muttered Tollen harshly. He took a quick swallow from his canteen. 'From the noise Monroe was makin', I'm surprised we ain't had the whole bunch of 'em on our necks before now.'

'You could be right. I don't think so. But maybe we ought to move out before anybody else decides to come along.' A flinty edge of anger marked his tone. 'Better waken Monroe if you can. He's had more sleep than the rest of us.' Without waiting to see if his order was carried out, he moved over to where his horse was hobbled, threw on the saddle, tightened the cinch under the animal's belly.

Lander bent over the inert form in the blanket, shook Monroe's good shoulder and waited impatiently until the other rolled over on to his back, his eyes flicking open. Monroe mumbled something unintelligible under his breath, would have rolled back on to his side had not Lander said: 'We're pullin' out, Verge. Better get on your feet if you're comin' with us. If not, we're leavin' you here.'

'Like hell you are,' snapped the other thickly. Somehow, he got to his feet, stood swaying unsteadily for a long moment, face drawn and white with pain. Then he moved over to where the horses stood, lips compressed into a tight line. He almost fell off balance as he neared the horses and they reared up in sudden alarm at the unexpected movement.

'Watch yourself, Monroe,' snapped Venner angrily. 'You want everybody in the hills to know where we are and that we're movin' out?'

'I couldn't help it, goddamit!' flared the other. He sucked in a sharp intake of air as pain lanced through his shoulder muscles. The rough bandage was bloodied a little as the wound began to bleed again. There was a dull throbbing in his head as the blood rushed through his temples and it was difficult to walk properly. Using his good arm, he managed to get the saddle on, aware that the rest of the men were seated on their mounts, watching him, making no move to help him, and this made his anger flare more fiercely within him. Gritting his teeth, he climbed up stiffly into the saddle, gripped the reins with his good hand and forced himself to ignore the stabbing spasms of agony that cut through him, burning inside his shoulder. He knew that it had not been an idle threat that Lander had made. If they thought they could silence him, they would leave him there, rather than be hampered by an injured man. The thought came to him then that if he managed to stay with them until they reached the place which Venner had picked out for the cache, his life might be more secure. Now, if he were left behind for the marshal to find, he could tell them nothing, whereas once he knew the location of the hide-out for the gold, they would never dare to leave him to fall into Fergus's hands.

He clung to his mount with his knees as they moved out, forming into a single file, heading up a twisting, narrow trail that seemed to climb through the coarsely tangled undergrowth right to the summit of the mountain, angling around huge outcrops of stone, smoothed and weathered by long ages of time.

They crossed a stretch of eroded red sandstone gullies and cat-claw to another bubbling creek, splashed across it and moved upgrade for the best part of a mile, riding slow because in places the trail was so narrow that their legs scraped the rock on either side and in others, the ground to their left shelved away so quickly that there was a drop of almost two hundred feet yawning at their side. One slip and it meant instant death for man and horse.

By the time grey dawn was streaking the sky, they were well up the steep wall of rock, out of the thick timber. Here and there were isolated growths of pine, none as large as those they had encountered further down the slope, but for the most part they were forced to rely on the outcropping rocks for cover. Riding at the rear of the column, swaying in the saddle, Monroe felt the sweat break out on his forehead, grow suddenly cold as the wind, sighing down from the mountain crests, flowed over him. He glanced down into the deep shadow of the abyss off to his left, wondered if that posse was awake and on the move yet now that it was growing light, and more to the point, if they were scanning these higher slopes, looking for movement.

They're bound to spot us from down there now that we're out in the open, he thought tightly. *Why the hell did Venner have to come this way? There must be a better way up the slope, one giving more cover.*

Wiping the sweat from his forehead, he

felt the dizziness sweep over him and for a moment the whole world seemed to spin around in front of his twisting vision. With an effort, he closed his eyes momentarily, held them that way for a moment, then opened them, sucking in a deep breath, forcing his heart into a slower, more normal, beat. God, but his shoulder hurt. What the hell had Venner done to it while he had been unconscious? Maybe the other had made sure that some poison got into the wound when he had taken that lead out of him. He felt a little shiver go through him. Even if Venner hadn't done that, even if he had done everything he could for him, it often happened that a man died from blood poisoning after having a bullet taken from his body, even by a qualified doctor. The thought scared him and he tried to put it out of his mind altogether.

Ahead of him, Venner had suddenly stopped. Monroe edged his mount forward until he was just behind Lander.

'What is it?' he asked sharply. 'Somethin' wrong?'

Venner's voice drifted back to him. 'There's the trail. Better stick close. It can be dangerous.'

Monroe glanced in the direction of the

other's pointing arm. In the pale light, he was able to make out the Flats almost directly ahead of them, where three deep crevasses angled in from different directions. There were clumps of Spanish sword, long spear-like leaves that were the very devil for horses, slicing their feet as they moved through.

Tollen looked distastefully at the brush, said: 'You mean we've got to try to ride through *that*, Sage?'

'Only way through.'

'It'll be hell to navigate.'

Venner tightened his lips, but kept his voice under tight control. 'Yeah, the whole thing is hell. But we've got the gold and I figure you'll all ride through hell just to keep your hands on that. Now keep quiet and let's ride. We've got to get through there without leavin' a trace. I wouldn't put it past Fergus to trail us as far as this. But nobody in their right minds will reckon on us goin' through there.'

'Where's it goin' to take us, once we do get through it?' asked Borge.

'You'll find that out when we get there.' Venner turned in the saddle, moved his horse slowly towards the Spanish sword, walking the animal letting it find its own pace as it tried to find a way through the savage growths which could slash an animal's feet to ribbons within minutes. Monroe's horse shied at the growths as he urged it forward. Quite suddenly, he felt a desperate urgency to get out of this terrible country. Why couldn't they have headed south while they had been ahead of that posse? It had been obvious that with their tired horses those men would never have caught up with them before they'd crossed the border. Venner had something on his mind, something he wasn't telling the others. Monroe was suddenly very sure of that.

Their horses limping through the bushy tangle, forcing an almost continuous circling, they eventually reached the far side of the Flats, struck into timber again. Here, the air was green and cool, had not picked up any of the rising heat as yet and Monroe sucked down great gasps of it, striving to ease the pain in his lungs and chest. When he could spare the breath for it, he cursed savagely to himself.

'How much further do we have to go, Venner?' he called loudly. 'I'm about all in.'

Venner did not bother to answer. Then,

ten minutes later, they swung around a bend in the trail which had been nothing more than a game run ever since they had crossed those treacherous Flats and in front of them, set against a backdrop of rugged rocks, was a tumble-down shack. It looked to Monroe as if it had been deserted for twenty, maybe thirty, years. One side had sagged as the foundations had collapsed and the wall bulged outward as if punched by a mighty hand from inside the building.

'This is the place,' said Venner quietly. He reined up, then swung down from the saddle, looped the reins over his mount's head and walked forward.

'You sure this place is safe?' muttered Borge as he did likewise.

'Safe enough,' replied the other. 'Even from renegade Indians.' He ducked his head and went inside the shack. Supporting himself on his good arm, Monroe levered himself from the saddle, winced as he hit the ground, then forced himself upright. The narrow stretch of open ground in front of the cabin was screened by foliage and it looked impregnable to attack. He guessed that a few men could hold off an army here. He followed the others inside. There was little furniture inside the shack. A couple of iron bunks shoved against the back wall and a plain wooden table with three rickety chairs clustered around it. Weakly, he sank down on to one of the bunks, stretched out his legs in front of him and eased his torn shoulder a little under the rough bandage.

'You goin' to take another look at my shoulder now that we're here, Venner? I got a feelin' it ain't healin' right.'

'I'll attend to it when I've got time,' muttered the other. 'First thing we got to do is bury the gold and money. Then we'll have time for other things.' There was a dry, callous note to his voice and Tollen laughed harshly.

'That's it, Sage. The loot first, then men later.'

Venner swung on him, his right hand moving towards the gun at his belt. Then he paused, smiled thinly. 'Ain't no sense in quarrellin' here,' he continued thinly. 'We're all in this together whether we like it or not. Until the hue and cry has died down, we just have to put up with each other.'

Fergus rode at the head of the party as they moved on along the twisting trail which was all but concealed by the thickly tangled foliage. They had picked up the two men who had made camp further along the track and were now headed up towards the low ridges that thrust themselves out of the face of the rock just beyond the point where the belt of green timber ended. From then on, almost as far as the eye could see, the ground was rocky, but more open and he reckoned they might have a chance of picking up the trail of the five men. Swinging across a shallow creek, they scoured the further bank for prints, found those of five horses and moved after them.

'They're still close,' said Sharkey as he leaned forward in the saddle, pointing to the muddy ground and nodding, 'I'd say that one of them was badly hurt.'

'I'm sure I hit one as they headed out of town,' Joel affirmed. 'Might slow 'em up a mite, but not enough for my liking.'

They slanted up through the timber, found a small, almost invisible track that cut through the trees, followed it along its winding length and finally came to the spot where the five outlaws had made camp. Sharkey nodded to where the grass had been flattened said grimly: 'If we'd come on we could have caught up with them here. Might have taken them by surprise.'

Joel shook his head emphatically. 'They'd

have one man on guard all the time. If we'd tried anythin' like that we'd have run into an ambush, lost a lot of men. They could cover every direction of attack from here without exposing themselves to our fire.'

Daylight was beginning to brighten now. Down below them, the black shadow of the hills that lay over the plain was beginning to shorten. Almost like a dark, velvet blanket being rolled up, thought Joel inwardly. Their horses were going slower here, more carefully, treading warily as the ground dropped away from them in places while in others the rocky walls crowded in on both sides, forcing them to ride in single file. As he led the way, he probed the slanting shadows with his keen gaze, aware that this was excellent country for drygulchers, knowing that it was quite possible those men had left one of their number behind to watch the trail.

Dipping and rolling in sharp, upthrusting swells, the savage, primeval country stretched in front of them and they found themselves riding a long, curving sweep of land that moved steeply upward towards the higher ridges. Glancing back into the valley beneath them, Joel was able to make out the tumbled confusion of rocks and boulders, slowly being touched by the sunlight which broke like a mighty, soundless wave over everything, sweeping away the shadows of night.

A mile and they came on the Flats. Joel paused, sat with his arms folded over the saddlehorn, surveying the desolate country. Then, turning his head, he said to Sharkey: 'What do you think, Jeb?'

'Hard to be sure. They could have pushed through that Spanish sword, but it ain't likely. Difficult thing to do at the best of times and in broad daylight. But in the dark, it's well-nigh impossible.'

'Then you reckon they cut over in that direction?' Joel pointed to the long canyon, sides composed of a kind of smooth, volcanic rock.

'Seems likely. That will bring them around the other side of the range. By now, if they made good time, they could be miles away.'

'That's what I figure.' He paused, looked once more at the rapier-like growths that barred their path to the right. Even if the outlaws had gone in that direction, they would never find them in that expanse of rock and scrub. There were a thousand places where men could hide, too many to be searched by the men he had.

'What do we do, Joel?' asked Cornell from behind him. 'Go on, or turn back now?'

Joel paused, then shrugged. 'We have to turn back,' he said reluctantly. 'We don't have a chance in hell of findin' them in there.'

'Never figured you'd give up as easy as that, Marshal.' Sharkey turned his head and looked at him in mild surprise.

Joel gave a thin, tight-lipped smile. 'I ain't givin' up, Jeb. But I figure these *hombres* have decided to cache that loot somewhere up here until they reckon it's safe to split it up and then each man will head for the border. When that happens, I'll be ready for 'em. I'll get that money and gold back if I have to trail 'em all the way to the border and across into Mexico.' He wheeled his mount with a savage jerk on the reins, headed back along the trail.

'There must be a better way of doin' this apart from sittin' here in town twiddlin' our thumbs,' Jeb Sharkey said tightly. He was watching Joel Fergus, who sat at the desk in the marshal's office, checking through the wanted posters in his desk. Across from him, Cookie Henders scanned the pictures closely, shook his head each time as he placed them back on the desk.

'You're sure none of these is the critter who stayed the night at your place, Cookie?' Joel asked at length.

'I could be mistaken, Marshal. But I don't think so,' nodded the other. 'He didn't look much like any of these. How'd you know you'll have a picture of him here?'

'I don't. But there's a chance he may be among these. I only caught a fragmentary glimpse of them as they rode out of town. If you don't see him here I'll get in some of the tellers and employees from the bank to go through them.'

'Virginia Kern reckons a stranger stayed at the hotel that night too,' broke in Sharkey. 'Reckon he might have been one of them?'

'Could be. Ask her if she'll step along to the office when she can. We may have better luck with that one.' He stacked the pictures together and placed them in a neat pile on the desk in front of him. 'All right, Cookie, that's all for now.'

'Sorry I couldn't be of more help, Marshal.'

'Not your fault. I already figured that they weren't well known in this part of the territory. From what I've heard, none of them wore masks when they held up the bank. They must have been pretty confident they wouldn't be recognized to do that.'

'Yeah, that's right.' Cookie wrinkled his forehead in thought. 'You show me any of those *hombres* mixed up in that hold-up in Abilene?'

Joel grinned faintly. 'Only got one here,' he said. 'I showed you it along with the others, but you didn't recognize it.'

'Guess I was wrong about that then,' said the other in a disappointed tone. 'I had them figured for the same bunch and–' He broke off as the street door opened. Sharkey came in and behind him was Virginia Kern.

'Was there something I can do for you, Marshal?' she asked.

Joel nodded. 'I want you to take a look at some pictures I have, Ma'am. I'd like you to tell me if you recognize any of them.'

'You think that the man who stayed at the hotel the night before the bank was robbed, was one of the hold-up men?' Her eyes widened just a little.

'I didn't say that,' Joel countered. He handed the pile of notices to her. 'But if you do recognize any of these men as that guest of yours, I'd be obliged if you'd let me know. Take your time. There's no hurry. I want you to be quite sure if you do see anyone.'

Virginia Kern seated herself in the chair which Cookie Henders had just vacated and began turning over the notices slowly, glancing through them. Cookie gave a brief shrug of his shoulders, turned and went out into the street. For a moment the staccato sound of his footsteps sounded on the boardwalk outside the building, then faded swiftly into the distance.

'Why do you think that man was one of the bandits, Marshal?' asked Virginia Kern. She did not look up as she spoke.

'I've got the feeling that these men played their hand very cleverly. I think they rode into town separately, maybe even came in from different directions so as to arouse no suspicion. A bunch of men riding in together would have been noticed at once.'

'I see.' She nodded gently, almost frowning. A moment later, she pointed at one of the posters. 'This is the man who stayed at the hotel. I'm sure of it. He was a little cleaner than this, well-dressed, but I'm certain I'm not mistaken.'

Joel stepped forward, took the poster from her outstretched hand. Behind him, Sharkey said: 'Is it the man you thought it was, Marshal?'

Tautly, Joel nodded. 'It's him all right,' he

muttered grimly. 'Sage Venner. He led that raid on the bank in Abilene some months ago.'

'Knowin' who he is, does that help us in catchin' him?'

'Maybe,' murmured Joel musingly. 'An outlaw is often a man of habit. I figure that Venner is the same. He planned most of his robberies with the same kind of thoroughness that he did with this one. Somehow though, I get the feelin' that he's lookin' for the time when he can pull out, get someplace across the border and spend the rest of his life livin' off his ill-gotten proceeds.'

'I guess he could do that right now, judgin' by what he got from the bank.'

'I think so too. Even if they split it equally five ways, it's still a pile of gold. Now he's got it, he'll take no chances of bein' caught. He'll rest up there in the hills until he judges it's time, and then light out for the border, takin' his share with him. My guess is they'll split up when they've done the share-out.'

'That won't make our job any easier,' muttered the other grimly.

'No. But now we have this information, we can telegraph all of the law enforcement officers from here to the border to keep a look-out for Venner and the others. I want to wire Abilene for pictures of the rest of the gang too. Check if anyone can identify them as havin' stayed the night in Benson.'

'Is there anything more you want me to do, Marshal?' asked Virginia Kern, getting up from her seat.

'Thank you, no. You've helped us a lot as it is.' Joel showed her to the door, then came back into the office. 'Jeb – I want you to go along to the telegraph office and send this message for me to the sheriff of Abilene. I'll send the other messages myself to the lawmen south of here.'

He scribbled the message quickly, handed the piece of paper to the deputy. When the other had gone, he sat back in his seat, hands clasped behind his neck, staring up at the ceiling. He was still staring at it when the door opened softly and Jenny Tindel came in. He half rose to his feet, but she motioned him to remain seated. 'I know how tired you must be, Joel,' she said softly, her voice rich and warm. 'You can't have had much sleep for two nights. I brought you something to eat.'

'Thanks, Jenny.' He pushed himself forward on to the edge of his chair as she placed the food in front of him. 'I must admit I do feel mighty hungry.'

'I baked the pie myself,' she told him modestly, sitting down in the chair opposite him. 'I want to see you eat it all. The coffee is hot.'

He ate with relish, feeling the girl's gaze on him, but giving no sign that he noticed. Not until he had finished, pushing the empty plates away from him did she speak again. 'Joel – I met Jeb Sharkey coming into the office as I left. He said something about you knowing the identity of one of these bandits.'

'That's right, Jenny. A man named Sage Venner. He led that raid on the bank in Abilene. Also got a lot of stage hold-ups to his credit although whether they were all carried out by this gang, I doubt.'

'And what do you have to do now? Go out after them again?' Her tone bore an anxious note.

He nodded slowly. 'I have to, Jenny. That's my job. But I'm not ridin' up there into the hills after them. That would be futile. I'd never find them in there even if I had a hundred and fifty men at my back. I intend to wait them out. Sooner or later, they're goin' to figure that the heat is off and when that happens, they'll make a break for the

Mexican border. That's when I intend to make my play.'

'But how will you know when they've left the hills and headed for the border?'

'I've got men watchin' every trail down from those hills. They have their orders, not to try to stop them. I can't spare enough men to be sure of takin' them in when they try to break for the border, so they'll warn me the minute they cut and run for it.'

'And then you mean to trail them, no matter how far that trail leads?' It was as though the girl could read the thoughts that lived in Joel's mind.

'I'll find them,' he said flatly. 'And I'll bring the money back with me. As for those outlaws, they'll come dead or alive. Either way will be all right by me.'

'Be careful, Joel,' she said softly. She filled his coffee cup again with the steaming brown liquid. 'These are dangerous men. They'll wait and shoot you in the back if they get the chance.'

'I'll watch for them,' he promised. He sipped the coffee in a ruminating silence. 'Could be though that they'll run into trouble even before I catch up with them. I'm warnin' every sheriff and law-officer between here and the border, sending them the descriptions of the men we want. There'll be a net spread to catch them when they make their break.'

Jenny smiled down at him as she gathered up the dinner plates. When she had gone, he sat back in his chair, his hat tilted forward over his eyes, listening dreamily with a part of his mind to the sounds outside in the street. A solitary rider went dusting by, the sound fading quickly into the distance. The sound of singing reached him from the saloon across the way. Deep in his mind, he wondered whether the net he was placing around Benson, would be close-meshed enough to trap men like Sage Venner and those who rode with him.

4

TREACHERY

Sage Venner paced the room, pausing occasionally to listen to the night sounds outside the shack. Behind him, Tollen lifted his canteen to his lips, let the brackish water trickle down his throat before giving a disgusted sound and hurling the waterbottle away from him. It hit the floor and skidded into one corner.

'We'll be in fine shape if we have to stay here much longer,' he rasped. 'I say we've hidden out long enough. Six days and you still reckon that marshal will be waitin' down there at the bottom of the trail.'

'Shut up!' Swinging on him, Venner bit the words out sharply. 'We pull out as soon as I give the word – not before. Is that clearly understood?'

After a surly silence, Tollen said: 'You know, Venner. I've been thinkin' these past two or three days. It seems to me that you've got more on your mind than tryin' to make sure we get clear over the border with our share of this gold. I figure that you're tryin' to find some way of seein' that there's only one of us left to take the pot and that one will be you.'

'Tollen. I've warned you. Keep your mouth shut if you can't talk sense.' Venner advanced on the other, his fingers resting lightly on the butt of his gun. 'I don't want to have to kill you, but if you make me, I will.'

Tollen pushed himself away from the wall, his face stiff with anger. 'That's how I had it figured, Venner. Well, I'm warnin' you. Give me just one reason and I'll kill you.' He squared his thickset shoulders, eyes blazing. The scar on his cheek burned a fiery red on his tanned flesh, only partly hidden by the six-day growth of beard. 'Maybe you figured out how to take that bank in Benson, but so far as I'm concerned, you ain't runnin' things any longer.'

'I'm runnin' this much of it,' Venner snapped through clenched teeth. 'We stay here until I say it's safe to pull out. You ride on down that trail now and you'll be a dead man before you reach the plain. Try to use your head, Tollen. By now, every goddamned sheriff and lawman from here to the Mexico border will have our descriptions and be on the look out for us. They'll have posses scouring the countryside lookin' for us. Even if we was to split up like we planned, we wouldn't get more'n fifty miles before runnin' into one of them.'

'We've only got your say-so on that. How will you know when it's safe? You ain't got second sight any more'n the rest of us.'

'Maybe not. But at least I'm tryin' to put myself in that marshal's place and try to figure out what he's likely to do. Now sit down and let me hear no more of this.'

Seated in the corner on one of the bunks, Monroe watched the two men closely. His shoulder still ached, but the stabbing pain had gone. Inwardly, he wasn't sure whether this was a good sign or not. If there was infection there, it could be either. 'What do you figure on doin' with me when you do decide to pull out, Venner?' he asked after a brief, uneasy pause.

The other turned. He said quietly: 'We'll give you your share and then it'll be up to you to make your way out of here as best you can. You got to see that, Monroe. That's the way we agreed on.'

Monroe gave a thin smile. The other had tried to make his words sound convincing, but there had been a false note to them, grating a little on the ear, a tone that stopped his next question before he asked it. He sank back on the bunk, teeth pressing into his lower lip as he struggled to move his arm. There was a numbness spreading down into it now. He could still move his fingers, but the rest of the limb, and his shoulder, seemed to be utterly lifeless. Soon, he reasoned, he would have no feeling in his hand. Then, if it spread into the rest of his body–

With a shudder he forced the thought out of his mind. He was probably just letting his imagination run away with him, he told himself fiercely. Settling himself into a more comfortable position, he closed his eyes and tried to sleep. The tension inside the shack had grown more electric as the days had dragged themselves by. Most of the others, he knew, had figured that at the most they would be forced to hole up there for three, perhaps four, days; certainly no longer. Now they had been cooped up here for six days and inevitably they were getting on each others' nerves, suspicions were growing in their minds and they had got to the point where each man watched the others, fearful of a bullet in the back before the gold was shared out among them. He, too, was puzzled why Venner wanted them to remain there for so long. He could not visualize that marshal and his men having sufficient supplies to stay around for this length of time watching the trail. By now, he had probably been in town for three or four days, giving up the chase as hopeless, relying on the telegraph for sending a warning out to the other towns further south.

Reaching up, he rubbed his forehead. There always seemed to be a film of sweat beading his skin now, even when the air was cold and he had the uncomfortable feeling that he was becoming more and more fevered as time went on. He wondered whether to mention this to Venner, then decided against it.

Outside, it was dark, but there was moonlight filtering in through the glassless window, giving sufficient light for them to see each other clearly. At night, they dared not risk having the lantern lit, although there was still enough oil in it to last them for as long as they were likely to be there. He listened to the others bickering among themselves, seeming to hear the sounds as if from a tremendous distance. Nothing about the prospects for tomorrow seemed good for any of them, he pondered. He spent a minute thinking it over in his mind. Maybe if they had lit out for the border right away instead of following Venner's orders and coming here first, they would have been in San Antonio by now, spending their money on wine, good food and the dark-eyed *señoritas* there. The thought made him feel warm all over.

A few moments later, Venner made a move towards the door which hung askew on broken, rusted hinges. From the far side of the room, Tollen said sharply: 'Where are you goin', Venner?'

'Just figured I'd take a look around before we turn in for the night,' said the other. His face was tight but expressionless. 'Any objections?'

'None. Just so long as I go with you,' muttered the other. 'That gold cache is out there in the rocks. I wouldn't want you to get gettin' ideas of diggin' it up and ridin' out, leaving us here.'

Venner made to reply, then checked the harsh retort that rose to his lips. With a sudden gesture he said: 'Very well, then, if you don't trust me, come along.' Giving the other a bright-sharp stare he led the way out of the shack into the yellow moonlight.

At the far edge of the clearing they paused, stared down into the dark-green shadow of the belt of timber almost directly beneath them, but perhaps half a mile distant. There was no sign of a camp fire there and from this vantage point it would have been possible to spot the flickering glow of a fire all the way down the sheer slope of the mountain, unless it was hidden right inside the thickest part of the timber.

'There ain't nothin' there,' Tollen said after a brief pause. 'I didn't expect to see anythin'. By now, Fergus and his possemen will be sleeping in a soft, warm bed, while we have to wait here until you've made up your mind.'

'Now see here, Tollen,' said Venner sharply.

'No–' cut in the other, swinging slightly. 'You see here, Venner. You've been the big man of this outfit for so long that you reckon you just have to give the orders and we all jump like rabbits to carry 'em out. Well, I'm sick of jumpin'. I want my share of that gold right now. Then I'll take my horse and ride on out. If I get myself caught on the way then it's my bad luck, nothin' to do with the rest of you.'

'And if they make you talk, tell them

where we are,' put in the other, his voice deceptively mild. 'What then? You expect us to let you go before we're ready?'

'Before *you're* ready, you mean,' snarled the other viciously. 'You've got the idea of takin' it all for yourself. Ten thousand dollars ain't enough for Sage Venner, the big man of the outfit. Maybe you figure that dead men tell no tales and if that posse could ride up here and find four dead men, they might not look any further even if they didn't find the gold. Well, nobody's goin' to kill me.' He jerked the Colt from its holster, levelled the barrel on the other, hissing through his teeth: 'Now move to the cache and start diggin'. And I wouldn't try to yell to the others. There ain't no bullet that can stop me before I put one through your heart. Just remember that if you start gettin' any funny ideas.' He jerked the barrel of the gun slightly towards the rocks piled high on the far side of the clearing, some fifty yards from the shack. 'Now move. And don't try anythin'. My finger is awful itchy on this trigger and believe me, I only need the slightest excuse to kill you.'

'You won't get away with this, Tollen. I should have known that you would try to pull a trick like this.' For a moment, the thought of action lived in his eyes and the set of his jaw. His fingers were stiffly spread just above his gunbelt. Then he forced the thought away. He looked for a moment down the barrel of the gun lined on him. It was absolutely still, stone steady. No use to gamble. Not now anyway.

Moving slowly to the rocks, he paused, felt the gun hard in the small of his back.

'You know where it is,' Tollen said harshly. 'Dig it up, divide out one-fifth. I don't figure on takin' more than what I have comin' to me.'

Grimly, Venner pulled the heavy rocks away from the hole, rolling them to one side. When he had finished, he shovelled the loose dirt away, revealing the tops of the wheat sacks, just visible in the pale moonlight.

'That's better,' said Tollen. There was a note of exultant satisfaction in his tone. 'Just bring them out.'

Venner's right hand closed on the top of the nearest sack. Pulling it out of the dirt he set it down on the ground in front of the other. Then he reached in for the second sack, gripped it more tightly than before, hesitated, then swung swiftly and unexpectedly, levering himself up on to his knees at the same time. The heavy sack caught Tollen on the wrist, knocking the gun from his grasp, sending him staggering backward. He made a low growling sound deep in his throat as he fell, hitting the rocky ground hard, his wind coming from his lungs in a long whoosh.

Without pausing to go for his gun, Venner uncoiled in a long, low dive at the other, snatching at a rock as he fell, aiming a savage blow at Tollen's head, kneeing him in the stomach as he went down. Tollen grunted and floundered, drawing up his legs as he sagged under the crush of Venner's weight and tried in vain to throw him off. He fought for breath as Venner chopped down at his throat with the side of his straightened hand, fell back limply. For a split second, Venner relaxed his vigilance, but it was the chance that Tollen had been waiting for. The blow on the throat had taken the wind from him, but there was still plenty of fight left in him. He swung upward with one knee, catching the other on the shin, hurling him back by the sheer force of the blow. Off balance, Venner fell back, hit the rock behind him, his head striking it with a stunning blow. Groggily, he fought to hold on to his buckling consciousness. Through tear-dimmed eyes, he saw that

Tollen was now on his hands and knees, scuttling forward. Squaring up, he prepared to meet the other's onslaught, saw almost too late that Tollen did not intend to move towards him. Instead the other lurched sideways. His outstretched hand reached for the gun that lay among the rocks a short distance away, the metal gleaming faintly in the moonlight.

Tollen's fingers closed around it, lifted it as he dropped on to his side, bringing the weapon up, his finger whitening as he squeezed on the trigger.

Tollen's eyes gleamed with anticipation, lips drawn back over his teeth. He started to say something, but in that same instant, now back on balance, Venner threw himself sideways and down, heard the other's gun roar, felt the breath of the bullet as it passed through the space where his head had been a split second before, shrieking off the rock into the night. His own gun was out now as his hand slashed down for it. He drew and fired in the same single, fluid movement, the deadly stiletto of flame tulipping out of the darkness in front of Tollen's stunned frozen gaze. The bullet took the other high in the chest, tearing through clothes and flesh and lungs. He reared up on to his knees, his body jack-knifing as the lead struck him, driving him back almost on to tiptoe. His Colt tilted forward to his fingers, the barrel pointed at the ground in front of him. Desperately, calling on every last ounce of strength in his body, he strove to lift it again, for one last, despairing shot at the man who lay in front of him. The gun exploded with a savage roar, but the bullet kicked into the dirt less than a foot from his face as he toppled forward, arms and legs crushing under his weight.

Very slowly, Venner got to his feet, walked over to the other, turned him over with the toe of his boot. Tollen's arms and legs fell limply by his side and his head lolled stupidly to one side, the eyes open and staring, already covered with a faint glaze where the moonlight caught them. His lips were drawn back in a savage snarl of defiance, even in death.

There was a sudden movement near the shack and the door swung open on creaking hinges. Lander and Borge came out, their guns in their hands. They stood for a moment peering about them in the moonlight, then spotted Venner and came over, holstering their Colts as they saw the dead body of Tollen lying on the ground at the other's feet.

'He was goin' to grab off the lot for himself and ride out tonight,' Venner said quietly. 'He had a gun on me, forced me to dig it out for him. I managed to hit him on the arm with one of the sacks, but he dove for the gun, would have killed me if I hadn't got him first.'

'Couldn't say that he wasn't warned,' grunted Ed Borge. He rubbed the bristles on his face, making a small rasping sound in the stillness. 'What do we do with him now?'

'Leave him here,' Venner said sharply. 'If the coyotes don't get him, that posse will once we pull out.'

'You changed your mind about leavin'?' asked Lander. The suspicious look on his face was beginning to fade slowly. He still kept his hand very close to the gun at his waist, not sure of what had happened.

'We have to pull out now,' Venner moved back to the shack. 'Those shots could've been heard all the way across the mountain. Sound travels well at night.' He threw a quickly speculative glance at the moon. 'I reckon there are still six or seven hours left to dawn. If we divide out the gold now, and then pull out, we can be well on the way to the border before daylight. We'll split up at the bottom of the trail.'

'And Monroe?'

'We can't take him with us. We'll have to leave him here.' There was a hard note in Sage Venner's tone. 'That shoulder of his is infected. He can only last another day or so before the poison spreads to the rest of his body.'

'What about his share of the gold. A dyin' man ain't got no use for it,' grunted Borge.

'You've got a point there,' nodded the other. The thought had already occurred to him but he had not, for obvious reasons, wanted to be the first to bring it up, specially now that Tollen was dead.

'Can't say I like the idea of shootin' him down in cold blood,' mused Lander. 'Still we don't want him talkin' to the posse if they do get here before he dies.'

'Not much chance of that,' said Venner decisively. 'He's a lot worse than even he knows. I've seen this happen before. Man with a slug in his body. Even after it's got out, infection gets into the wound and within a week he's dead. Get your horses ready. We'll split the money and ride on out. By the time he realizes what has happened, it'll be too late for him to do anythin' about it.'

Pale yellow light revealed the inside of the shack. Drowsily, Monroe remembered the shots that had sounded just outside the hut, recalled Lander and Borge getting hurriedly to their feet, snatching up their own guns, and running outside. He had waited for them to came back for what seemed an endless period, but which could have been only a few minutes. Then, straining his ears, he had just managed to pick out the low murmur of their voices in the distance, but it had been impossible for him to make out any of the words.

Something had happened, he told himself. Either Tollen or Venner had been killed and now the others were trying to decide what to do. Even as the thought ran through his mind the danger of his own position was born to him. He threw back the blanket with his good hand and tried to stand up, but with the movement, it was as if his head would fly apart. He heard the sound of horses from the rear of the shack.

It came to him then that they were pulling out, that they had divided the money among them and were leaving him to his fate. There was his own gunbelt lying over the back of the chair on the other side of the long table if only he could get to it. He tried again to stand, gritted his teeth as the blood throbbed painfully through his temples. The room tilted and swayed in front of his stultified vision and it was all he could do to remain on his feet.

Savagely, he forced himself to move, shuffling his feet in the dust on the floor as he moved forward. He stumbled against the table, felt it move a little under his weight as he sagged forward, resting himself on his good arm, the other one now completely useless, even his fingers refusing to obey him. He lay there for several moments, drew in a rasping breath, head lowered like that of a bull in a rage. His body swayed as he felt the strength draining from it, but he knew he had to move, that it was essential he should reach the door and see what was going on outside.

There was blood on his shirt front now. This was the first time that the wound had bled for five days, but he scarcely noticed it. Lurching forward, he staggered against the chair, caught hold of the gunbelt, forced air between his clenched teeth and slowly withdrew the Colt from the holster, gripping the weapon with convulsive fingers as if afraid that at any moment he might lose his grip on it. Another shuddering breath – one which throbbed as it distended the muscles of his throat and chest. His mind was busy, working ahead to what might have happened. The sound of horses moving around on the rocks came to him again, urging him on. He reached the door in ten shuffling steps, leaned against it as he peered out, pushing his sight through the yellow haze of moonlight that flooded into the clearing facing the shack.

There was an intense trapped feeling in him. The sound of horses travelling quietly was clearly audible now and jerking his head around with a savage wrench of tortured neck muscles, he saw the three men move their mounts out from the shadows near the tall rocks, edge them across the clearing to where the narrow trail angled down out of sight into the brush.

'Get back here, Venner – you bastard,' he yelled hoarsely. 'You ain't runnin' out on me.' He wasn't sure that the man in the lead was Venner. For all he knew it might have been Venner who had been killed, shot by Tollen when he tried to prevent him from riding out.

A harsh voice which he did not recognize bellowed something from the darkness and through his dim vision he saw one of the riders wheel in the saddle, jerk up his right hand. There was the blue-crimson flash of gun-flame lancing out of the darkness and the slug tore a long sliver of wood out of the doorpost less than a foot from his body.

Veins throbbed in Monroe's throat as he called on all of his remaining strength, forcing the gun in his hand to lift, the barrel lining up on the fleeing men. He loosed off one shot, thought he saw one of the men stagger and lurch in the saddle. More pressure on the trigger. Sound hammered again against the stillness. It bucketed along the looming wall of rock, but the shot itself went wide, tore into the bushes. He fired again, but the men were almost out of range, on the very edge of the clearing. Before he could bring more pressure to bear on the trigger they had dipped down out of sight and the crackle of their mounts through the dry brush faded swiftly.

Monroe's arm lowered limply to his side. His eyes were wide, staring things and there was more sweat beading his forehead, trickling down his cheeks and dripping from his chin. He hung there in the doorway of the shack, listening to the deep, ominous stillness which had closed down over the hills, swaying on his feet like a tall slender tree caught in a high wind. Still the gun hung in his hand.

Slowly, very slowly, he lifted his head, stared off into the moonlight and it was then that he noticed the shape huddled near the rocks where they had buried the gold. From that distance, it looked like a pile of old sacks, but he knew it was a man even as he thrust himself unsteadily from the doorway and staggered forward, feet slipping on the rough, uneven ground. He fell to his knees several times and finished the last twenty yards at a crawl, heaving his bruised body forward by means of his legs, thrusting them over the ground, knees and elbows torn and bleeding. Two yards from the fallen man and he paused, head thrown back, staring at the other stupidly, dazed and silent. As a man in a dream, he wormed his way forward the rest of the way, lay on his side and heaved the man over, looked down into the staring, sightless eyes that peered up at the star-strewn heavens, already glazed in death.

It was Tollen. Weakly, he sank back on to his haunches. He might have expected that, he thought dully. Somehow, Venner had turned the tables on him, shot him down. Now the other three were heading out for the border. As the thought passed through his mind, he thrust himself up on to his feet, seized with a sudden desperate anger. Somehow, he reached the rocks, pale white in the moonshine, scrabbling in the dusty earth with his fingers. The hole was empty. All of the loot was gone.

For a long moment, there was a white-hot fury in him. Maybe Venner had been planning this all along, he thought savagely; the first step in getting all of the gold for himself. Tollen dead, himself left behind to die; and as for the two men who had ridden with him – sooner or later, they would get careless and they would end up as Tollen had, shot in the back, their bodies dumped somewhere along the trail to Mexico.

Slowly, the fury subsided. He became aware of his own predicament. Maybe if he managed to get to his own mount, he could ride down, head back into Benson and give himself up. They would get him to a doctor then, save his life. It would mean prison for him, he realized that; but anything was preferable to staying here to die. He sucked in a deep breath. Whatever happened, before he died, he would make damned sure that Venner and those other two did not get away with this. They would regret that they hadn't stayed to kill him.

Reaching the edge of the Flats, Joel Fergus reined up and lifted the rifle in his left hand, signalling to the five men behind him to halt. He held the rifle by the shank of the butt as he had all the way up the steep slope, with his finger close to the trigger; it was cocked and loaded. If they had run into an ambush on the way at close quarters the shooting would have been fast and he had made sure that he had all the edge he could possibly give himself.

Pausing for a moment, his eyes now accustomed to the moonlight after the darkness which had existed under the trees in the timber belt, he glanced about him, then turned and waved up the rider immediately at his back. The man edged his mount forward with his knees.

'You're sure those men came up this way and then cut across through that scrub?' he said softly.

The Indian nodded his head soberly. He pointed off to where a very faint trail, more of a game run than a track, wound through the Spanish sword and mesquite. 'They went there,' he said, nodding.

'You got any idea where that trail leads?'

The Coyotero gave another nod. 'Old shack high up among rocks. Men can make camp there and not be seen.'

'Sounds like the sort of place Venner would make for,' said Sharkey, his voice drifting out of the moonlight. 'I figure that must be the way they went when we lost them the last time we came this way.'

'Question is,' went on Joel, 'are they still there? They could've pulled out by now.'

'If they had, the boys watchin' the trail down below would've seen them.'

'I guess so,' Joel nodded. He was not quite as convinced of that as Sharkey apparently was. He knew the sort of men he was dealing with, cunning men who would not have stayed alive and out of prison as long as they had, if they hadn't planned everything down to the last detail. They would have guessed he would have left men watching most of the trails down and they would have done their best to slip through the cordon of men he had placed around the foothills. Still, there was the possibility that they were still up there even after six days.

He reached a sudden decision. 'Let's go,' he said tightly. He gestured to the Coyotero to lead the way, knowing that the other would be able to read sign even in the moonlight and across rough country such as this.

They moved steadily through the brush patches, pausing for a moment when they reached the other side, the Indian bending in the saddle until his head almost touched the rough ground, then he straightened, motioned them on where the sign of horses angled sharply around an outcropping of stone. The others followed in single file, shale crunching underfoot, sliding beneath the horses as they climbed. This was bad country, Joel reflected; just the sort of terrain that suited men like Sage Venner.

The previous afternoon, the Coyotero had arrived in Benson and ridden up to the marshal's office, asking to see him. There was little doubt that he had been one of the men that Joel had chased off into the hills after the ruckus in town a little over a week before and he had been on the point of tossing the other into jail, when the man had mentioned seeing white men ride up through the hills, men who had carried heavy sacks tied to their saddles. Listening to the other's story, Joel had been convinced that the man had been telling the truth. Shrewd questioning had elicited the information that the Coyotero had trailed the men to their camp on the same night as he and the posse had camped in the foothills, that one of the men had spotted him watching them and had hunted him away.

These Indians were notorious liars as Joel well knew, but in this case he was certain that the man had been telling the truth. There had been no word from any of the men he had watching the trails down from the hills and he had called together four of his deputies and they had ridden out of Benson within the hour, pushing their mounts hard to get into the hills before nightfall.

The going became rougher the more they progressed towards the higher ridges, the surrounding country was ideal for ambushes and Joel felt the muscles of his stomach tighten as he peered about him, still keeping a tight grip on the rifle. Almost two hours after leaving the Flats, they passed through a maze of tumbled rocks and narrow creeks which angled into a wide plateau, curling in from every conceivable direction. The ground here was slashed by midnight shadows where deep, narrow crevasses cut it into ribbons of rough rock, gleaming faintly in the moonlight. Overhead, the tall summits, nearer now, still loomed over them and he had the feeling that the whole weight of the mountains was shifting down on him. With an effort, he forced the feeling from his mind.

He was so absorbed in his study of their surroundings that he failed to notice the Coyotero had reined up his mount, holding up his hand for silence. His own horse stopped suddenly as it came up against the Indian's pony and Joel swung sharply in the saddle.

'The shack,' said the Coyotero softly. He pointed through the thin fringe of bushes directly ahead.

Joel bent forward in the saddle, saw the clearing just beyond the brush and set against the solid wall of rock which dominated the entire scene, the tumbledown shape of a shack, details slowly materializing from the shadows as his eyes took in the outline of the building. The place seemed deserted on the face of things, but he had long since grown to distrust first impressions. Invariably they eventually proved to be wrong and if those men were shacked up here, then to step out into the open would be to invite a bullet.

'You reckon they're still there?' murmured Sharkey. He edged his mount alongside Joel's.

'Could be. They won't be expectin' trouble unless they have a man as look-out further back along the trail and he's given them the warnin'.'

The Coyotero shook his head. 'Nobody watching trail,' he stated positively.

'Then we may be able to take 'em by surprise,' Joel nodded. 'Work your way around the perimeter of the clearing. Don't fire until I give the signal. We'll call on them to surrender first. If they realize they're surrounded they may do so.'

'Wait.' The Coyotero's voice was a soft murmur. Slipping from the saddle, he moved forward a little way into the brush, went down on his knees, then rose and came back. He said quietly: 'There's a dead man over there by the rocks.'

'Dead?' Joel dismounted, moved over to the other. 'Are you sure?'

The other nodded, pointed a finger. Brushing aside the strand of thorn in front of him, Joel narrowed his eyes, squinting through the moonlight. A moment later he was just able to make out the mass of shadow that lay sprawled close to the distant rocks, some way from the shack itself.

'Listen,' Joel said, going back to the others. 'It looks to me as though they've shot it out among themselves, quarrelling over the gold. Follow me and be ready to shoot if anythin' moves inside that shack. Sharkey, take one man and move around that way.'

The other nodded, slid from his saddle, loosened the gun in his holster, motioned to Foster and edged out into the open. There was no move from the shack to indicate that they had been seen. Slowly, Joel let his pent-up breath go in slow pinches, then moved out with Cornell and the Coyotero behind him, making no sound as they cat-footed it across the stretch of open ground in front of the shack.

Motioning Cornell to move over to where the body lay in the lee of the rocks, he edged towards the wall of the shack, pressed himself tightly against it, inched towards the open doorway, the Colt cocked, thumb on the hammer, holding it back. At the door, he hesitated for a moment, then kicked it in with his foot, stepped swiftly through the opening, eyes flicking around the shadowed interior of the hut.

There was a sudden movement in one corner and he swung the gun instinctively to cover it, saw the man lying on the low bunk. Moonlight glinted on the weapon in the other's hand and Joel rasped tautly: 'Drop it!'

A pause, then the gun clattered to the floor. Keeping the barrel of his own weapon levelled on the other, Joel went forward very slowly, stared down at the man on the bunk, saw the rough bandage, blood-stained and dirty, that bound up the other's shoulder.

Joel recognized the other at once from the pictures he had received from Abilene a couple of days before. He smiled thinly at the other. 'So they rode out on you, Monroe,' he said grimly. 'Somehow, I expected that.'

'Yeller rats,' muttered the other, speaking through clenched teeth. 'They shot Tollen and took all of the money and gold for themselves.' His eyes burned with a red, feral gleam. 'They're headed out for the Mexico border, Marshal. Rode out less than three hours ago. I tried to stop 'em, but with my shoulder it weren't no good. Think I may have winged one of 'em.'

Sharkey and Foster came in, looked around them, then holstered their guns. 'No sign of anybody on the other side of the hut,' Sharkey said. 'But there are only a couple of horses there.'

'The others pulled out,' Joel said harshly,

his tone grim. 'We must've missed 'em on our way up. Which way did they go, Monroe?'

'That way.' The other pointed a shaking finger in the opposite direction to that which the posse had taken on its way up. 'Venner was damned sure you'd have men watchin' the trails. He wanted to stop Tollen from pullin' out and takin' his share with him, reckoned that if Tollen was caught, he'd tell you where the rest of us were. The two of them went out to look around. Then there was this shootin' and Lander and Borge ran out. They never came back. Reckon Venner must have changed his mind about ridin' out. I heard them takin' their horses, but by the time I made it to the door they were pullin' out. I went to take a look at Tollen but he was dead when I got to him.'

'Three hours,' said Joel quietly. He rubbed his chin thoughtfully. 'Even if they get through the cordon, we'll manage to overhaul them before they hit the border.'

'What are you goin' to do about me, Marshal,' asked Monroe in a thin, whining tone. 'This shoulder of mine ain't been gettin' any better since Venner tried to fix it. I need a doctor real bad.'

'We'll get you back into Benson and have the doc take a look at you,' Joel said tightly. 'If he manages to patch you up, I've no doubt you'll swing for your past actions. Heard that some men were killed in Abilene when you pulled that robbery there.'

Cornell came in a moment later. He jerked a thumb behind him. 'That *hombre* back there looks like Tollen,' he said thinly. 'You can see where they had the gold cached. It's all gone now. Guess the others must have it with 'em.' His glance fell on Monroe. 'What happened to him?'

'Poisoned shoulder by the look of it,' Joel said roughly. 'Reckon they didn't want to be hampered by takin' a wounded man along with 'em. Besides, there are only three of them now to split the loot.'

'Venner and the others headed out?'

'That's right. About three hours ago. They cut down a back trail which is why we didn't bump into them on our way up here.'

'I think we're wasting time now,' Cornell said. He turned abruptly and made for the door, halted as Joel called him back.

'There's no big hurry,' said the marshal quietly. 'We know the trail they took and it won't be difficult for our guide here to follow it. It's a mighty long haul to the frontier and I'm pretty certain that's where they're heading. They'll never make it in less than ten, maybe fifteen days, even if they push their horses to the limit. We'll take this *hombre* into town first, get all the information we can from him, and then head out after those others.'

5

CAST A WIDE LOOP

Joel put down his coffee cup and worked with cigarette makings. Looking at him, thought Sharkey, it was hard to believe that there was still that deep anger working in him against those men who had robbed the bank in his town, for Benson was Joel Fergus's town. He was responsible for law and order being kept and whenever anything like this happened – which was not often – he took it as a personal affront and a challenge to himself.

Leaning forward, Sharkey said quietly: 'That *hombre* over at the doctor's, Joel. You reckon he was tellin' the truth about the trail the other three took?'

'He wasn't lyin',' Joel said. He lit the cigarette, pulled the smoke down into his lungs. 'He'd got no call to lie about it. Those three had left him there to die and run off with his share of the gold. He'd do anythin' he could to see them roast in hell.'

'When do you figure on headin' out after them?' Sharkey put down his empty cup, got to his feet and went over to the window, looking out into the early morning light which flooded over the dusty street.

'About an hour,' Joel said. 'I want you to stay in town, look after the place while I'm away. I'm takin' the Coyotero with me to follow sign, and Cornell too. The three of us should make good time.'

'Only three?' Sharkey's brows shot up in surprise.

Joel shrugged. 'No sense in takin' more. There's only three of them.'

'Sure, but are you figurin' on giving the Coyotero a gun?'

'I reckon so. Ain't any whiskey out there in that desert.' Getting to his feet, he went over to the rifle rack, took down one of the Winchesters, checked it, feeling the buttered smoothness of the sliding parts, laid the weapon on his desk, then broke open a packet of shells. He thrust a couple of handfuls into his pockets.

'Cornell's over at the saloon if you want him,' Sharkey said. 'Could be the Coyotero is with him.'

Joel rubbed an aching hip, then crossed over to the door, stepped out into the street and made his way across to the saloon. It was still cool inside the place although the heat head was rising swiftly now that the sun was up. Cornell stood at the bar. He glanced round as Joel moved beside him, motioned to the bottle in front of him, signalling to the barkeep to bring another glass.

'Figured you'd be over, Marshal,' he said, leaning his weight on the bar. 'You ridin' out after those outlaws?'

Joel nodded. 'They won't be able to take a straight trail to the border. Too many towns in the way with posses out scourin' the surroundin' country for them, and Venner will know it. I figure we ought to reach them a day or so before they get to the border.'

'And if we don't?' There was a serious question in the other's tone.

Joel's lips drew back in a tight grin that was more of a snarl than a smile. 'Then we ride clear over the border after them. I don't mean to come back without the three of them. Dead or alive, it depends on them. If they give themselves up, all so well and good. If they decide to fight, then by Godfrey, that's all right with me.'

'Who's going, Marshal?'

'Just you and me and the Coyotero. We'll

be enough for those three.'

'You sure? I've heard they're all mean men with a gun.'

'Maybe so, but this is goin' to be the end of the trail for that bunch. I'd say the rot set in when they busted up at the shack. Maybe if they'd stuck together, they'd be somethin' to contend with, but not now.'

He finished his drink, set the glass down on the counter. 'Better get your horse and some supplies,' he said after a brief pause. 'It's going to be a long ride and across that stretch of desert, we don't know when we'll find water again.' He turned for the door, paused: 'Better take a rifle from the office too, and some shells. There's a box on my desk. I'll have a word with Jenny Tindel and then pick up the Coyotero. We pull out in three-quarters of an hour, before the sun gets too high.'

He strode along the street, paused for a moment outside the telegraph office, then pushed open the door and stepped inside. Jenny was seated at the desk. She glanced up, surprised, as he entered, then got to her feet and came around the edge of the desk, right up to him. Her keen gaze did not miss the bulging pockets filled with shells and he knew that she had guessed their meaning.

'You're riding out after those three out-laws, aren't you, Joel?' It was more of a statement than a question, but he nodded his head slowly and gripped her elbows.

'Somebody has to go after them and bring them in to face trial,' he argued gently. 'And I guess that as marshal here it's my job.'

'Are you taking the posse with you?'

'Just Cornell and the Indian. I figure that three of us will be enough. Besides, a small party will travel faster than a big one and I don't want to be seen until I'm good and ready.'

'Dad says that they'll head for the border now that they've made their decision to run for it. There's no other place that's safe for them after this. Do you think that you have any chance at all of cacthing up with them before they cross into Mexico?'

'I don't know. I think we have, but if not, then I'm quite prepared to go into Mexico after them.'

'But you can't. You have no jurisdiction whatever over there. Suppose that the authorities stop you? You know as well as I do that they have very little liking for us.'

'I know that. But if they don't know why we're there, they won't suspect anything. Besides, I'm determined that those men

136

aren't going to spend the rest of their lives living off the proceeds of murder and armed robbery. I'll bring them back, either in the saddle or lying across it.'

She shook her head slowly, her eyes clouded. 'I think you're a fool to do this, Joel. Now that they've got out of this territory it's nothing whatever to do with you. You've warned the other law officers south of here and it's up to them to keep a sharp look out for these men, try to stop them from getting through. How do you know that they won't resent you treading around on their territory, trying to steal their thunder by going after these outlaws?'

Joel pursed his lips, shrugged his shoulders. 'That's a risk I'll have to take,' he murmured. 'I'm leavin' Jeb Sharkey here as my deputy. He'll keep an eye on things while I'm gone.'

'How long will you be away, Joel?' There was a definite note of anxiety in the girl's voice which he did not fail to recognize.

'A month possibly, maybe a little longer. A lot is going to depend on how good a time we make and whether they decide to stand and fight or not.'

'I wish you'd see this thing in its proper light, Joel.' She looked up at him suddenly, her face shadowed. Standing straight, she came up to his shoulder, but now she seemed oddly smaller, her figure slight and feminine, lips turned down a little at the corners in her seriousness.

'That's what I am tryin' to do, Jenny. And the only way I can see it is what I'm doing now. Those men are murderers, they can't be allowed to go scot-free. Besides, I'm taking with me one of the best trackers there is. Venner and his companions don't stand a chance of getting away from us. Even if they try to backtrack to steer clear of the towns along the trail.'

'Then there's nothing I can say that will make you change your mind?'

'I'm afraid not, Jenny. I'm sorry.' He was frowning as he spoke.

'I suppose you think I'm talking foolishly?'

'No, but you're talking like a woman, letting your heart rule your head. You just can't sit back and let these men go free.'

'All right.' She nodded her head reluctantly. 'But take care, Joel. From what I've heard they are dangerous men. They haven't stayed alive as long as this at their trade by being slow with a gun.'

'I know. I'll be careful.'

She let her gaze rest on his face for a long

moment, then stepped very close to him, stood on tiptoe, placed her hands on either side of his face, drew it down to hers and kissed him briefly on the lips. He put out his arms to tighten them around her waist, but she had stepped back, eyes dark now, a faint smile curling her lips, lifting the corners of them.

He paused to look at her for a long moment, then turned on his heel and walked out into the glaring sundrenched heat of the street. Slowly, he made his way along the boardwalk towards the middle of the town. Several of the people he passed on the way spoke to him. At the corner of the intersection, Ellis the banker, stopped him.

'Is it true that you brought in one of those bandits who robbed the bank, Marshal?'

'That's right. He's at the doctor's right now.'

'Oh, did you have trouble bringing him in?'

'No. He must have caught a bullet when he rode out of town after robbing the bank and one of the others took it out without taking the proper precautions to sterilize his knife. There's an infection in the wound and the doctor ain't sure whether or not he can pull him through. He's in a bad way.'

'I'm sure I've got no sympathy for him,' said the other harshly. 'Those killers deserve all they get. What about the others?'

'One of them was shot during a quarrel. We found his body up in the mountains. The other three had ridden out before we got there. Seems no doubt that they're headed for the border.'

'Don't you intend to get a posse ready and go after them then?' demanded the other excitedly. 'Once they cross into Mexico they'll be beyond the reach of the law and–'

'Calm yourself down, Mister Ellis,' Joel broke in. 'I'm ridin' out in half an hour's time. It's a fortnight's journey to the border from here even if they were able to ride straight there, which they're not.'

'I'm afraid I don't quite understand.'

'It's quite simple. I've already passed word along by telegraph. They'll know this and they have to steer clear of any towns along the trail just in case they run into any of the posses out looking for them right now. There's a real big manhunt going on for those three at this minute.'

'But if they should slip through and get to Mexico it–'

'It won't help them at all,' Joel broke in. 'Because I'm not going to rest until I've caught up with them. If they cross into Mexico, then you can be sure that I'll go in after them.'

'Do you think that would be wise?' queried the other doubtfully. 'I mean they have no extradition agreement with us. They may try to stop you bringing them back out.'

'They may,' Joel said easily. There was something in his tone that made the other pause, ask no further questions. 'Now if you'll excuse me, Mister Ellis, I've got to make some arrangements before I ride out.'

'Of course, Marshal.' The other nodded, wiped his sweating forehead with a red handkerchief. 'I'm glad to see that you're getting on with your job.'

All that he's glad about, thought Joel tightly, *is getting his money back. He doesn't care men are killed in the process.* He stepped down into the dusty street, crossed over and went into the law office, his spurs making faint jingling sounds in the stillness.

Cornell glanced up from his chair, then got to his feet. 'Saw you coming, Marshal,' he said. 'I got the Coyotero. He's ready to ride any time we are.'

'Good. Get him a rifle and some shells from the box.'

Cornell stared at him in surprise. 'You goin' to give him a gun, Marshal?'

'That's right. If he comes with us he gets a gun like any other deputy. I reckon he knows how to handle one.'

'Sure, I guess so.' The other looked dubiously at the Indian who stood near the door, arms folded, his features inscrutable. Cornell's expression said quite clearly that he didn't trust an Indian with a loaded rifle riding with him, but presently he shrugged, got a Winchester out of the rack and passed it over to the Coyotero. The other took it without any change in his expression, folded his arms around it.

Joel said: 'You're a deputy now. So long as you ride with us, you take your orders from me or Cornell here. You understand that?'

'I understand,' nodded the other. 'I use this gun to kill those three men?'

'That's right. If they decide to stand and make a fight of it, we shall have to kill them. We have no other choice.'

They went outside to the waiting horses. Joel noticed the saddlebags that were tied down to them. They would need these supplies before they crossed that great stretch of empty desert. Once they reached the other side, there would be places where they could obtain more. But it was at least a three-day journey before they came across any other sign of habitation. Inwardly, he wondered if Venner knew this. The indications were that he did. They way they had made their way so unerringly to that shack up there in the hills was clear enough evidence that he knew this country well. Most likely the man had fought with the Confederates during the war. There had been innumerable skirmishes here in those days. Men in the army then would know every trail through those hills, every isolated place where they could rest up for a while without running the danger of a surprise attack.

Five minutes later, they rode out of town, the dust settling slowly in their wake. When they reached the edge of the Badlands, the sun was already high over the horizon and climbing steeply to its zenith. Heat lay like a vast and smothering blanket over everything. In front of them, the narrow, partly obliterated trail was just visible, winding in and out of upthrusting outcrops of red sandstone, an indication of things to come. They kept up a steady pace during the morning, heading almost due south, leaving the rearing columns of the mountains at their back. Joel could feel the taut eagerness still in him, a force which drove him on, which would continue to drive him on, despite all of the dangers and discomforts, until he reached the end of this trail and three men stood in front of his guns.

Although they raked their spurs over their horses' flanks, the animals refused to be hurried. It was as if they sensed the discomforts which lay ahead of them and wanted nothing of it. He comforted himself with the knowledge that things would be just as bad, just as difficult, for those three outlaws and that if they tried to push their mounts beyond the limit, they would soon find themselves without horses.

Clattering in and out of the arroyos and stony gulches, rocks and pebbles scattering underfoot, bounding and rolling down the steep slopes they encountered, they continued through the rough country, heedless of any possible ambush.

Afternoon and there was a change in the weather. By now, they were well into the desert. Around them, as far as the eye could see, lay nothing but the harsh, glaringly white alkali dust, stretching away to the boundless horizons. A terrible land which would never be tamed by man. The sun, still a blinding glare in the heavens, was a diffuse disc, a strange and fearful thing. The ceaseless vibrant whine of the wind had risen in pitch, was shrieking softly in their ears, blowing directly at them out of the south, lifting the eddies of dust with it, boiling up the alkali until it was as though waves were rippling over it, filmy clouds scurrying over the rocks which showed through the dust.

Their horses were soaked in lather and sweat, rolling in their stride, their breath sobbing heaves which could be heard quite clearly even above the high-pitched keening of the wind. Joel screwed up his eyes and lidded them a little as he tried to peer ahead. The full fury of the blinding grains of sand lashed the exposed flesh of his face and hands, worked its way between his clothing and flesh. A deep breath filled his lungs, the hot air going down into his chest like fire. The storm had brought an added danger. It would swiftly obliterate the trail and he doubted if the Coyotero could follow it. The clouds of dust blurred details, made it difficult for them to see where they were. He cursed savagely under his breath. This was the last thing they needed. It would slow down their progress, possibly wipe out the trail utterly. Then there would be a further waste of time before they succeeded in picking it up again.

It was not until late afternoon that the storm abated. Slowly, the last breath of wind died and there lay a great stillness around the three men. Where the trail had once existed, there was absolutely nothing but a river of sand and alkali, ankle-deep, through which their mounts thrust their feet reluctantly.

Straightening up in the saddle, Joel removed the reversed neckpiece from over his nose and mouth, thrust it back into his pocket. Turning his head, he stared at the others out of red-rimmed eyes. His face was sore and tender where the multitude of irritating grains had scoured and abraded the flesh.

'Guess it's over for the time being,' he remarked. 'We'll push on until dark, then scout around for the trail again in the mornin'.' Already the sky was clearing miraculously. Blueness appeared through the white haze which had obscured it most of the afternoon. The light of the glowing sun, low in the west, flooded the desert with a crimson brilliance.

Dejection settled heavily on Joel as he sat tall in the saddle, shading his eyes against the setting sun, gazing out over the savage wildness that lay ahead of them, facing the inescapable fact that they were only at the beginning of their journey. This land wanted nothing of Man, rejected him with everything at its disposal. The dunes were swarming with a vicious, poisonous life which the desert had made its own; rattlers and copperheads and other species of equally poisonous snakes. Even in the old days, the Indians kept well to the north, skirting the area. All around them, the vast stretch of the desert, that which they had crossed, and that over which they still had to travel, was void and silent in the darkening twilight, showing no sign of movement right to the shimmering horizons, no indication whatever of the presence of any living creature.

He pointed off to one side where a low ridge, the only upthrusting spur of rock in the extending flatness, showed against the skyline. 'We'll make camp there,' he said quietly.

There was little comfort for them that night.

The claypan gulches which ran off in all directions along the base of the ridge were dry and cracked with the heat and drought. There would be little water until they had crossed the Badlands and they were forced to try to sleep with the dust itching and irritating their skin, rubbing into their limbs with every movement they made.

Joel felt bone tired as he stretched himself out under his blanket. There was no wood or brush around in this desolate region to enable them to build a fire and they made cold camp. The temperature dropped swiftly once the sun went down and the moon rose, and even under the blankets it was icily cold.

Joel lay on his back in his blankets, but he did not sleep, not for some time, thinking of Sage Venner and the two men riding with him, out there someplace, heading for the border. Around him, the silence was deep and intense and he could make out the breathing of the two men lying on the rock nearby and the faint sounds of the horses as they moved their position on the bare, rocky ledge.

It was going to be a bad trail, following those three men, he thought to himself, turning events over in his mind. He did not doubt that he would catch up with them some time, and he felt sure they would fight rather than surrender themselves. Inwardly, he hoped they would fight. Only by destroying them would he be able to forget the anger against these men. He knew exactly what he would do. He was sure, even though he had told Cornell that he wasn't certain.

He rubbed a hand along his face where it had been scorched by the sun and torn by the howling storm of alkali. He didn't have to go through with this. He didn't really have to do anything as far as Venner and the others were concerned. He had done all that the law strictly required of him, caught up with two of those critters, one dead and the other probably dying. He had sent out the warning all the way along the trail south and it was now up to the other lawmen there to watch for these men. But he knew he would go through with this, no matter what they came up against along the trail, no matter how long it took. There was no sense in lying here and arguing with himself. His mind had been made up that moment this gang had robbed the bank and succeeded in evading capture.

Something will happen soon to end it all,

he reflected – one way or the other. And that was good, because it ought never to have started. If he hadn't been so tired after that fruitless night's ride into the hills after those goddamned Coyoteros, he would have taken notice of the warning that Cookie Henders had given him about the stranger who had put up with him during the night and who had asked a lot of funny questions about the bank, pumping the other for information. He would have checked with everyone else in town who might put up strangers riding in late at night and the picture would have been clear to him before those men had had a chance to put their plan into operation. He had been fooled all the way along the line. Maybe it was this, more than anything else, which brought the sharp sense of anger which he could not ignore. He knew that if he rode back into Benson without these three men, then he would have to live the rest of his life with the inescapable fact that he was a failure. Even if he never made that mistake again, it would always be there, haunting him. It would be far better for him if he turned in his badge right away, rather than go on being a lawman.

Most of the time, until he fell asleep, these

thoughts continued to pound through his head and their effect was to heighten the feeling of urgency in his mind to the point where he could scarcely contain it.

The three outlaws rode through the narrow cut of a sundried creek. They had caught the tail-end of a sandstorm which had blown across the desert, slowing their progress and Venner's mind was once again filled with a sense of rising apprehension. The border with Mexico was still a long way off, several hundred miles even if they had been able to move in a straight line. As it was, word would have been telegraphed to every town and hamlet along the route, warning them to be on the look out for them and he knew they would have to work their way around these places, be on the look out every single moment of the day and night once they crossed this wasteland of desert and dry scrub.

The bed of the creek twisted along a shadowed course, between high walls of red rock, and over everything lay a gravelike silence that ate at their raw nerves and caused the hairs on their necks to ruffle uncomfortably. A little way behind the other two, Lander rode with his shoulders hunched tensely, eyes flicking from side to side, expecting trouble every moment. With an effort, he forced himself to relax, thinking: *A shoulder is no protection against a .45 slug.*

He was beginning to wonder whether Venner knew just what he was doing. They had been riding now for three days, ever since they had dropped down out of the mountains and cut across the Badlands. Their water was low now and they had found none during the whole of that time. Another day of this and their position would be desperate.

Thinking about it, he became irritated. Gigging his mount forward, rubbing the back of his hand over his cracked lips, he called: 'You sure we ain't just ridin' around in circles, Sage? Seems to me I recognize that mound yonder. Looks like the one we passed this mornin'.'

Venner turned slowly in the saddle and gave him a peculiar studying look before speaking. 'How the hell can we be ridin' in a circle if we keep the right direction by the sun?' There was a biting note of sarcasm in his tone.

Lander flushed. He wanted to say something more, but knew he would get the worst of any argument with Venner and clamped his lips tightly together.

'There's some higher ground yonder.' Borge pointed. 'Reckon we could make camp there, Sage. Some brush, too, for a fire. I'm sick of makin' cold camp.'

'We'll make a fire if I say so,' Venner snapped. 'Don't forget that by now Fergus will be on our trail. And he won't be wastin' time either.'

'You reckon he'll come?' asked Borge.

Venner gave a quick nod. 'He'll come,' he repeated. 'And he won't spare himself until he catches up with us. We made a fool out of him, robbin' that bank in full daylight and he knows it.'

They reined up their mounts in the lee of the high ridge. Here, there was a wide, rocky overhang forming a shallow cave.

'Let's get a move on,' said Venner. He slid thankfully from the saddle, rubbed an aching hip, then climbed up on to high ground for a quick look around, before clambering back again to the rocky bottom of the draw. He nodded. 'May as well start a fire. Reckon nobody could see us unless they got right on top of us.'

He leaned his back against the rock face, watched as the other two gathered dry brush, made it into a pile. Lander struck a sulphur match, applied it to the dried grass, stood back as the flame caught, crackling through the tinder-dry vegetation. They broke out their meagre supplies of food and utensils from the saddlebags and while Lander sliced off salt bacon with a deft handling of his knife blade, Borge set some of their precious water to boil over the fire.

Fifteen minutes later, they ate their meal, ears attuned to the different sounds of the desert. The sun had gone down a little while before and the shadows had merged and blended over the face of the desert, bringing a blueness to the terrain. The air became cool and a breeze sprang up once more, sending little flurries of sand off the tops of the crests and dunes.

Borge absently poked at the fire with his boot. He kept his ear cocked to the country above the rocky overhang, then let his gaze flick to where his mount grazed on the coarse grass nearby, the wheat sack containing his share of the gold still securely strapped to the saddle. Switching his gaze to the other side of the fire, he caught Venner watching him closely from beneath lowered lids.

'How long do you figure it's goin' to take

to reach the other side of this doggoned desert?' he asked abruptly.

Venner gave his attenion to whetting his bowie knife on a smooth layer of rock, shrugged. 'Should have crossed the worst part of it by tomorrow night at this time,' he observed. 'Why – you got somethin' on your mind?'

'Seems to me we've got very little water left and there ain't no likelihood of findin' any in this god-forsaken spot.'

'We'll make out.' The other tested the edge of the blade with his thumb, then thrust the knife back into his belt. 'You reckonin' on leavin' us when we reach the other side?'

Borge felt a little tremor go through him. How the hell had the other known that? He forced a shrug. 'Could be. It's goin' to be too dangerous if we stick together. Any posses out there will be lookin' for three men ridin' together. One man on his own stands a much better chance of slippin' through.'

'Why the hell don't you come straight out with it and say that you don't trust us?' snapped the other harshly.

Borge grinned viciously. 'Maybe that's it,' he admitted. 'After what happened to Tollen and Monroe you can't blame me for feelin' that way. Seems to me that you've had somethin' on your mind ever since we rode out. If you see a chance of gettin' away with all of this gold, then by God you'll take it, even if it means shootin' Lander and me in the back to do it.'

For a moment, the other's hand dropped close to the gun at his belt, then he paused, lips drawn back over his teeth. 'I've warned you before about talkin' that way,' he muttered. 'Both of you. Can't you see that the only way to get through and into Mexico is to keep our heads. If we're suspicious of each other, always watchin' the next man, then we'll be easy prey to Fergus and his men.'

Borge put down his cup with a thud and his thick fingers toyed with it for a moment, then he said harshly and decisively, 'I still intend to ride off alone when we hit the other side, Venner. I wouldn't advise you to try to stop me. That was our agreement when we planned this and you're damned well stickin' by it.'

Venner tightened his lips, then shrugged. 'If that's the way you want it, then it's all right with me.'

'Good. Just wanted to get it straight.'

'You've got it straight.' Venner swung on

Lander. 'Anythin' like this eatin' you?'

'I think Ed's right. We ought to split up as soon as possible. That way, we have a better chance.'

Venner stared belligerently across the fire at the two men, then said through his clenched teeth: 'When you fall into Fergus's hands, you'll wish that you'd listened to me.'

The next day, there were dark clouds obscuring the sun when they moved out of their camp and the sky was greyly overcast. In spite of this, the heat remained, sucking all of the moisture out of their bodies until they felt limp and dehydrated, swaying in the saddle, peering into the gloom.

Glancing at Venner, Borge said: 'You sure you can find your way now, when there ain't any sun to find directions by?'

'I'll find it,' retorted the other. He hauled on the reins, jerking his mount's head around sharply, riding down along the creek bed, not once looking over his shoulder to see if they were following him. Lander glanced at Borge, saw the other shrug, then wheel his mount.

The creek banks flattened to a shallow flat that continued for a couple of miles. Far off, in the distance, the storm had broken over the low foothills that climbed up on the horizon and an occasional flash of lightning crisscrossed the heavens where the thunderheads lifted high into the sky. Venner pulled up the collar of his coat as he eyed the approaching storm. It would be on them before long, he reflected; but so long as it brought rain with it to damp down the dust, it might not be so bad.

The dark curtain of rain swept in swiftly from the southern horizon, crowding out the pale glow that marked the position of the sun behind the swarming clouds. Thunder rode with the storm.

'Keep ridin',' Venner called as he saw the others begin to slow. 'There's no shelter here.'

As he spoke, a savage gust of wind caught at his words, snatching them from his lips. A solid blanket of rain, large, heavy drops, struck them, beating on their heads and faces. Lightning flared savagely, followed almost at once by the roaring, cracking of thunder almost directly overhead. Venner gritted his teeth as he kept his head low, bending forward in the saddle, feeling the rain slash at him as the wind drove it directly at them. He knew of these sudden storms which started without much warning in the middle of this desert. They were rare occurrences, but when they did come, they represented nature in the raw, a primitive savagery which had to be experienced to be believed.

All three men were soaked to the skin within moments of the storm closing about them. Giant forces were at work around them. Savage lightning strokes which blinded them, the crackling roll of the thunder. Underfoot, the alkali had turned into a churning sea of muddy white through which their mounts struggled gallantly. Their legs sank into the mud and they floundered helplessly in places where the rocks had become covered with a thin treacherous film of it. Venner sat easy in the saddle, resting his horse as much as possible.

An hour passed and still the storm thundered and roared about them. The horses were reacting now to the savagery, rearing and pulling, panicking in spite of the tight rein holding them in.

'We've got to hole up somewhere, Sage!' called Lander harshly, rubbing his knuckles over his eyes where the rain, dripping from his hair, ran into them. 'We can't keep ridin' through this. The horses will break soon.'

'There's no place to shelter,' Venner shouted back. 'Use your head, man. We've got to keep goin'. I know these storms. They last for an hour or so and then pass over as quickly as they come.'

'I hope so.' Wind snatched the words from Lander's lips, whirled them away. He lifted his head, stared into the full fury of the rain, pushing his sight through the gloom which lay all about them. The desert seemed to have changed now out of all recognition. A sudden flare of lightning, behind them now, showed a dark shadow on the horizon and he strained to make it out, saw a few moments later through his blurred vision that it was a narrow belt of thick scrub, topping a ridge of ground that lay across their trail. He could just see also the isolated clumps of trees that showed beyond the tangle of dark vegetation.

Crowding their mounts, they rode with the thunder chasing at their shoulders and plunged into the rain dripping brush. Each blue-white flash of lightning was now a little further away and, turning his head, Venner saw that the storm was passing as swiftly as it had come and there were clear streaks of blue off to the south-east. A distant flash showed the swaying branches above them, sparkling drops cascading down on them.

Venner shook himself like a dog emerging from a river, threw back his head and stared up at the clearing sky. His lips were drawn back, baring his teeth in a savage grin. Rain ran down his face and streamed off his bearded chin. For long seconds he sat motionless. Then he gave a nod. 'It's movin' away like I said it would.'

They dismounted, stood in a huddled group, waiting while the storm cleared. Borge rubbed his cheek, felt his sodden clothing clinging irritatingly to his body, knew there was nothing he could do about it. This was not the first time he had ridden wet on the trail, and it was but a small price to pay for having all that gold. His thoughts turned to what it could buy once he crossed the frontier into Mexico. No questions asked there. The folk in the South were only too glad to get their hands on Yankee gold without bothering to inquire where it came from or how he had managed to acquire it. He grinned faintly to himself, then threw a swift glance at the tall, frock-coated man seated in the saddle a few yards away. What sort of thoughts and ideas were going through Venner's mind at that moment? he wondered tensely. Was he figuring how he could stop both Lander and himself from reaching the frontier alive, so that he could ride across with all of the gold for himself? It was impossible to tell, but if anyone did have thoughts like that, it would be Sage Venner.

'Think we have time to build ourselves a fire and dry out?' Lander asked suddenly. 'The horses are tired battlin' against that storm and—'

For answer, Venner urged his mount forward a few paces, fingers gripping the reins in a white-knuckled hold. His mouth was grim, eyes narrowed. It lacked an hour of high noon and now that the clouds were clearing rapidly away to the north-east, the strength of the sunglare was beginning to make itself felt once more. Heat closed like a muffling blanket around them and their wet clothing began to steam.

'We've got no time to wait up here,' said Venner finally. 'We go on.'

'I'd like it better if I rode in comfort,' Borge said harshly.

'I said we go on now.'

'I figure,' said Borge quietly, voice ominously soft, 'you've got a reason for wantin' to rush these horses right to the limit – us too.'

'I have,' said Venner. 'Three reasons, maybe more. Who knows how many men Fergus has in that posse which is trailin' us.'

'You don't *know* there's a posse there,' put in Lander.

'No? You figure he's sittin' back there in Benson, twiddlin' his thumbs, waitin' for somebody else to try their luck bringin' us in?' Venner shook his head deliberately. 'He's there, right behind us. Maybe a day behind, probably only a few miles. You rest up here and he's sure to find you.'

'That dust storm and now the one just past will have wiped out any trail we made,' interposed Borge. 'Even I know that.'

'Thinkin' like that is the reason why you'll probably be dead long before you get in sight of the border,' Venner said softly. 'You think that everybody figures things the way you do. Fergus is a crafty individual. He'll bring one of those Coyoteros with him as guide and they can smell out a trail across rock even if it's weeks old.'

Ed Borge looked about him deliberately, eyes veiled. He did not speak for a long moment, then he said: 'I reckon we've also crossed the Badlands, Sage. Like I said, I'm for ridin' alone. I suggest we separate here, give ourselves the best possible chance of gettin' through.'

'If that's the way you want it – go ahead.' Venner shrugged, made to turn his mount, then suddenly jerked, his right hand striking for leather. He had almost drawn the Colt from its holster when Borge's voice stopped him, froze his hand.

'Hold it right there, Venner.' Borge levelled his revolver. 'I guessed you'd do somethin' like that.'

Very slowly, Venner moved his hand away from the butt of the gun, let it drop back into its pouch. He said thinly through his teeth, eyes narrowed in frustration. 'What do you aim to do now, Borge? Kill me in cold blood?'

Borge grinned viciously. 'I reckon that's what you meant to do. Then there would be only two to share the money. And after that, you could take your time decidin' how to get rid of Lander here.'

'You're crazy. The heat out there in the Badlands must've gone to your head. Now put that gun away and ride on out if you'd prefer it that way. We don't intend to stop you. Guess I'd sooner you did go your own way. I wouldn't feel too safe with you ridin' at my back.'

'What about you, Lander?' Borge asked.

The gun barrel did not waver as he spoke to the other man, saw the hesitancy on Lander's face.

'I guess I'll stick with Sage,' said the other eventually. 'He was the brains behind the outfit when we hit that bank, and the other before that. I'll ride on out with him.'

'Suit yourself,' Borge said roughly. 'Only when the end comes for you, don't forget I warned you.' He let his gaze drift back to Venner. He knew instinctively that of the two, only Sage Venner was dangerous. He said sharply: 'Take your guns out real slow, Sage, and kick the shells out.'

'What the hell–'

'Do as I say, or I might change my mind and kill you here and now. I don't aim to be killed, Venner, that's all.'

'Now see here, Ed–'

'Don't say any more.' The hammer of Borge's gun clicked back ominously. 'Just do like I say and then ride on out. I don't want to see or hear anythin' more about you. If we reach the same place in Mexico, I'll walk by on the other side of the street.'

Venner eyed him closely for a long moment, then did as he was told, letting the cartridges drop on to the wet ground. 'I don't know what's happened to you, but it's somethin' I don't understand.'

'I'll bet you don't. I've been watchin' you since that night when you shot Tollen down and left Monroe back there to die or be picked up by the posse.'

'Damn it all, Ed, what else could I do? Like I told you, Tollen had a gun on me, would've shot me down in cold blood if I hadn't managed to take him by surprise. And as for Monroe, there was nothin' more we could do for him and he would only have slowed up our progress.'

'That's the way you tell it,' Borge said. He waited until the other's guns were empty and thrust back into leather. 'Now ride on out of here and keep ridin'. I'll be watchin' until you're out of sight. Then I'll go my own way and God help you if you try to follow me and hunt me down.'

Venner tightened his lips, made to say something, then bit down on the retort and snapped: 'Let's ride out, Lander. If this goddamned fool wants to throw his life away it's no longer any concern of ours.' His eyes were narrowed with fury; a rage that gripped him and forced the veins of his neck to purple and stand out under the skin.

'You won't get far on your own,' he said thinly. 'I'm tellin' you that right now.'

'Will you try to stop me, Venner?'

'You mean nothin' to me now.' Venner's voice was low, held in check somehow by an iron will. 'But I figure you've underestimated Fergus. He'll ride you down before you've gone two or three days' ride.'

'We'll see.' Borge jerked up the barrel of his gun, watched as the two men rode out, angling their mounts through the brush. The shadowy foliage swallowed them a few moments later but for minutes, Borge trailed them by sound, until the last faint noises of their horses died away to the south. The sun inched free of the last traces of cloud, the ground steamed and after a few moments, he wheeled his mount and headed west along the treeline.

He let his horse take its time, still worried a little about Venner. It was not like the other to allow him to get away with this. There was a good chance he would ride on for a mile or two and then either lie in wait for him near the trail or scout around until he ran him to earth. If he did that, Borge thought grimly, it would be either Venner's life or his own. Inwardly, he doubted if Lander would take any part in this. The other would bide his time and await the outcome, possibly hoping that they killed each other, leaving him the victor. Sweeping the surrounding terrain with a keen-eyed gaze, his hand not once straying far from the gun at his waist, he rode west, the sun hot on his back and shoulders.

6

DIVIDED TRAIL

Kneeling, Joel Fergus looked through the trees which lined the edge of the low ridge. Beside him, the Coyotero pointed out the marks in the ground where the mud had dried out in the sun, freezing the imprints of the horses. 'They split up here,' said the Indian softly. He spoke in liquid Spanish, moving his fingers over the sign. 'Two went that way.' Pointing due south, he got lithely to his feet, one hand still gripping the Winchester.

Cornell, moving up with the horses, said harshly: 'We don't have any idea though who the third man was who struck off to the west – or why he did it.'

Joel rubbed his lips, feeling the mask of dust caked on his scorched flesh. Once the storm had passed, they had made good time over the desert, riding through the night without pause, and he felt sure they were now only a day or two behind the outlaws.

'I reckon we know why he did it. These men don't trust each other now they have the gold. They'll head for the border along different trails, not only to make it more difficult for us, but also to better their own chances of getting there alive.'

Cornell pursed his lips. He made a smoke, lit it and dragged smoke into his lungs, his brow creased in puzzled thought. 'You wouldn't think it would be Borge or Lander who would ride off alone, would you?'

'Maybe not. I'd say that it's most likely to be Venner. By headin' west, he could then trail them by turnin' south a few miles away, come up on them when they least expected it.'

'You still figure he means to grab off all the gold for himself?'

'Don't you?'

Cornell shrugged. 'Makes sense, I guess. He was the brains behind the outfit and we know he shot Tollen back in the hills.'

The Coyotero moved forward a few feet into the brush, bent, picked up something from the ground, brought it forward. He held it out to Joel. 'Cartridge for a Colt revolver,' he said. 'There are more there.'

Joel looked down at the cartridge in the palm of his hand in surprise, then glanced over at Cornell. 'What do you make of that?' he asked.

'Looks to me as though whoever held the gun, forced the others to empty their revolvers. Evidently he wasn't takin' any chances of bein' shot in the back when he rode away.'

'No.' The Coyotero shook his head. 'This one stay here until the others rode away. The marks show his horse moved around a lot.'

'Still doesn't help us decide who it was,' Cornell said. 'What do you intend to do now, Marshal? Do we split up and trail 'em both?'

'No. We go after this one.' He poked a finger in the direction of the trail that angled west. 'We can then head across country and try to cut off the other two.'

With the Coyotero leading, they moved into the coarse brush, splashed over the first stream they had encountered in almost three days, and followed the sign up the bank and into the sparse timber. There was no sudden transition in the terrain here and for the most part the trees were stunted in growth, their branches bending close to the ground, so that their horses were forced to go more slowly, more carefully. At the top of the long, low rise, they paused and glanced back. Below them, they were able to make out the stretch of ground on the edge of the desert where they had found the divided trail, but all about them, there was no movement.

Daylight was beginning to fade as they hit the open country a few miles ahead, the ground dipping and rolling in long, gradual swells and they let their mounts run hard, making up the time they had lost. The cool evening breeze blew in their faces and the air smelled fresh and clean, and behind them their shadows ran longer and longer as the sun dipped in a sea of flame, finally vanishing in a great silent explosion beyond the hills to the north-west.

Afterwards, the land changed; became blue and still, with the smell of the hills and pines in their nostrils and the cool air taking the sting of the long day's heat from their bodies. Before long, Joel was having to concentrate to keep in the saddle. His eyes grew heavy for sleep. Repeatedly he caught himself swaying forward, dozing off in the saddle. A glance showed him that Cornell was the same. The Coyotero was still wide awake, but Joel had expected that. These Indians could travel for days with the minimum of sleep.

At length, they worked their horses through a thick stand of pines and cedars and dismounted. Here the brush was thickly tangled but there was evidence of a rider thrusting his way through. Branches had been snapped and the coarse grass trampled underfoot. The Coyotero moved deeper into the brush while Joel and Cornell made a fire.

When he returned a little while later, moving noiselessly out of the shadows, he said softly: 'He made camp back there, about ten minutes travel through the brush. Ashes cold, but I found these.' He held out the three cigarette butts for the marshal's inspection, his features inscrutable.

Joel nodded. 'That's one of them all right,' he said after a momentary pause. 'Could you tell how long since he pulled out?'

'A day maybe – not more,' said the other without hesitation. 'I followed his trail to the edge of the timber. He moved east.'

'That's almost certain to tag him as Venner,' murmured Cornell from the other side of the fire. 'He's cutting back to trail the other two like we figured.'

Joel said nothing. Inwardly, he was not quite as certain of this as the other was. It looked that way and there was certainly the lure of the gold which those two men would be carrying. But surely those two men would have considered the possibility of Venner trailing them, hoping to take them by surprise, and they would have the numerical superiority and one man could keep watch while the other slept. There was something here which didn't quite tie up, some tantalizing thing they had overlooked, but in his tired condition he could not think what it was.

Finishing their meagre rations, they unsaddled and spread their blanket rolls on the soft earth. While the Coyotero watched, the two men slept, nestled to their saddles for pillows, the drug of sleep overcoming them within minutes. Joel slept like a dead man for five hours, then woke to a touch on his shoulder. The Coyotero stood over him, pointed at the moon, indicating that it was his turn to keep watch. Moving silently to his feet, instantly awake, he nodded. The other stretched himself out on the thin layer of pine needles, was asleep in an instant. Settling his back against the trunk of a nearby tree, Joel stretched his legs out in front of him, listening to the soft, muted sounds of the night. The moon hung in the

174

heavens, remote and cold, touching every-thing with a pale silver gleam that was utterly without warmth.

Morning found them on the trail again, hungry, because Joel had wasted no time for warming the meat they carried with them. He knew he was driving them hard, that the Coyotero would make no complaint, but he was not so sure about Cornell. The other's face had twisted into a grimace when he had given the order to ride out without any warm food for breakfast, but he had said nothing.

By mid-morning, they were halted in a narrow valley. A few yards from the others, Joel Fergus sat square in the saddle, cuffed his hat on to the back of his head and ran his hand over his sweat-marked forehead. Then, folding his hands on the saddlehorn, he tilted his head back, slitted his eyes against the beating glare of the sun and stared up at the towering range that lay on their right, the great cliffs of red sandstone curving round until they almost blocked the trail ahead.

Cornell, powdered white with dust, pulled rein alongside him a moment later and hooked one leg over the saddlehorn while he dug in his pocket for the makings of a cigarette. He twisted the strand of tobacco into the brown paper.

'Only the one pass through those hills,' he observed. 'He must've made it that way unless he circled around the range.'

'Unlikely,' opined Joel thoughtfully. 'That would have taken another day on the trail at least and this man is in a hurry. From what the Coyotero says, he's travellin' fast. Either he wants to overtake the others, cut in on their trail and lie in wait for 'em, or he knows that we can't be far behind him and he's tryin' to outrun us to the border. Could be that he figures he's safe once he crosses into Mexico with that stolen gold.'

'You're still intendin' to go over after them if they do get to Mexico before we catch up with 'em?' queried the other thoughtfully as he lit the cigarette.

Joel nodded tersely. 'Ain't nothing going to stop me,' he said, his tone sharp. He eased his hip in the saddle. 'That trail there where it passes through the pass looks good cover for a dry gulcher.'

Cornell snapped his head up, glanced carefully ahead of them. 'You think he may be lyin' in wait for us up there?'

'Could be – I don't want to underestimate any of those three men, especially if it is

Venner. He's smart and he's mean. We know he must've reached these hills sometime yesterday if the Coyotero is readin' the trail right but if he spotted us at all, he wouldn't wait out here in the flat, he'd climb the slope to get a better view of the terrain.'

'So you reckon he's spotted us.' Cornell dragged smoke into his lungs.

'Even though we tried to keep dust down to a minimum, he could've seen it from up there.' He turned to the Indian, sitting patiently close by. 'Those tracks go right on up to the pass?'

The other gave a brief nod, pointed to the dust. In places, the stray wind had cleared the trail, but there was still enough for them to make out the imprints of a horse, the depth indicating that it had been travelling fast, even upgrade.

Setting their horses to the slope, they rode slowly, their hands very close to their gunbelts, eyes alert, searching the rocks and shadows for the faintest glint of sunlight on metal that would give them an advance warning of a man with a rifle lying in wait for them. Joel was especially alert. He rode tensely, eyes sweeping ahead, raking every inch of the trail and the huge, eroded boulders which overhung it. The glare off the rocks was a terrible, eye-searing glaze that sent stabs of pain lancing through his eyes and right to the back of his head. A lizard scudded from one concealing shadow to another, attracting his attention right away, his right hand moving of its own accord. He stayed it as his fingertips brushed the warm metal of the gun. He was getting too edgy, imagining too much. The rocks which studded the slopes on either side as the mountain slopes came crowding in on the trail, rolling down towards them, were so numerous and in places the clumps of tangled brush so thick that deep within himself, Joel knew the chances of spitting a drygulcher before his rifle spat death at them were slim indeed.

High noon and they were still inside the great sandstone bluffs. The trail had led them through the pass and now, in spite of the tremendous, crushing weight of the heat, Joel felt a little easier in his mind. The man they were trailing had not once turned aside from the trail. If he had considered hiding inside the rocks and waiting for them, he would have taken his chance some miles back when the terrain had been more in his favour. Here, the slopes were more open, smoother than before, with very few of the huge craggy boulders which would have provided cover for a killer.

Angling around a sharp bend in the trail, the Coyotero paused, reining up quickly. He dismounted as the others rode up to him, bent to examine the ground.

'What is it?' Joel called.

'The man has taken more trouble here to hide his trail,' said the other, straightening up.

They rode on slowly now, dismounting frequently, looking for more sign of the trail. It was soon evident that their quarry had taken a lot of trouble here. Possibly, thought Joel, he had suddenly realized that since the trail was so narrow here, but with occasional discrete fissures saddling down from the slopes where a rider might easily turn off, he must try to hide his tracks, try to give the impression that he had swung off the trail somewhere. But soon, the Coyotero spotted where a snapped twig on one of the overhanging bushes showed the fresh white scar of sapoozing wood and two hundred yards further on, they located the small branch with moist earth and sand clinging to it which had been used to drag behind the horse, wiping out the tracks.

'So that's how he did it,' said Cornell

grudgingly. 'I wonder who he was afraid of. Us – or those other two men.'

'We'll probably find that out when we catch up with him. He can't be too far ahead of us now.'

By mid-afternoon, they were working their way across a long, flattish ledge that stood more than two hundred feet above the narrow valley. They had made much better time since noon because they had not had to stop frequently now to search for the trail. After wiping it out for that stretch of perhaps half a mile, their quarry had evidently considered it useless to carry on and the tracks of his mount were now clearly visible.

A mile further on, where the ledge lifted sharply, Ed Borge crossed over to the jumble of rocks, glanced through the wide Vee between two of them squinting along the trail. He had set himself up on that stretch, knowing that here at least he had a commanding view of the trail which his pursuers had to follow to reach him. He had suspected they were close behind him for almost a day now, had driven his mount on to its limit. Shortly before noon it had become lame and now stood hipshot among the scrub to his right a couple of hundred yards away. It would carry him no further and the inevitable conclusion had been forced on him. He would have to stay here and fight. If he managed to stop the men following him, he could pick up one of their mounts and get clear to the border. He knew there could be only two or three trailing him. The dust cloud he had seen fifteen minutes earlier when they had climbed the slope to the ledge had been far too small to have been kicked up by many horses.

He wondered who Joel Fergus had got to ride with him. There had to be an Indian with them to have followed his trail so easily. Only a Coyotero could have spotted his tracks all of the way.

He watched as the men rode nearer. Through the obscuring cloud of dust which shrouded them, he was able to make out Fergus now, riding second in the line. He did not recognize the man bringing up the rear, or the other in front, except that he was an Indian. He sucked a gust of air into his lungs, drawing his lips back over his teeth as he lifted the Winchester and laid the barrel carefully in the Vee of the rocks, squinting along the sights. They had made better time than he would have thought possible. Evidently they had decided to ride after the single man first, unless Fergus had brought a big posse with him and detailed the others to ride on after Venner and Lander.

At first, he had considered pulling up into the hills, hoping that perhaps the three men might ride on without seeing him, but he had instantly dismissed the thought. With a lame horse, he would not be able to get very far and he did not know this stretch of country. For all he knew, he might be fifty miles or so from the nearest human habitation where he might find another horse and some grub. Grudgingly, he watched the Indian lead the other two men. He'd sure done some mighty fine tracking to get them here as quick as this, without missing the sign. He clenched his teeth tightly. He ought to have known better than to try to blot out his trail. Those damned Coyoteros could follow a man over solid rock in the darkness.

He rubbed the back of his hand over his eyes where the sweat, dripping from his forehead, threatened to blind him. He'd have to get that marshal first. He would be trouble either way, so he figured to draw a bead and drop him first of all; then try for the Indian before he got under cover.

Inwardly he did not relish the thought of that redskin tracking him through these rocks, particularly as he saw now that the Coyotero carried a rifle. Trust that marshal not to miss a single trick. An Indian with a rifle was a deadly combination.

Lying full length on the rocks, he forced himself to breathe slowly, to ease the rising tension out of his mind. Everything was going to depend on the first two bullets, one for Fergus and the other for the Indian. He did not anticipate having much trouble with that deputy if the other two were out of the way.

Settling himself, he brought the butt of the rifle to his shoulder, squinted again along the sights. Another few minutes and they would both be within killing range of the weapon. It would be fatal to fire before they were close enough. Taking his time, he watched as the trio edged forward along the plateau, approaching the spot where the trail bent sharply before rising towards the ledge on which he lay. That would be the moment, he decided, just as they rounded the bend. He waited, forcing patience into his mind and body. Whatever happened, he must not hurry this first shot, give them the chance to drop under cover. More sweat popped out on his forehead and began its slow trickle towards his eyes, running into his brows. With an effort, he resisted the urge to shake it away. Another ten yards, reasoned his mind. He had the foresight lined up on the narrow trail at the point where it turned sharply, waiting for the Indian to ride into view, then Fergus. His tongue ran around his dry lips eagerly and his eyes held a feral gleam.

The Coyotero came into sight, riding slowly, evidently watchful and wary, expecting trouble at any moment, eyes peering against the harsh sunlight for the first signs of it.

Borge grinned viciously. The first indication they would have of his presence would be the slug that knocked Fergus from his saddle. Then a second shot for the Indian. After that, he would take care of the deputy bringing up the rear of the party. He would be clear out of this country and in Mexico before anyone knew what had happened, before the three bodies were discovered, or anyone thought to come and look for them.

It was this feeling of confidence which proved to be his undoing. He saw the marshal's mount move into view, got a quick glimpse of the other's broad shoulders in his foresight, blinked away the sweat that ran into his eyes at that precise moment and involuntarily squeezed the trigger.

The shot whiplashed at the very instant that Fergus caught the sharp gleam of sunlight on the barrel of Borge's rifle. Instinct saved him. Wheeling his mount back towards the rock face, he dropped forward in the saddle, heard the wicked hum of the slug as it cut through the air where his shoulders had been a split second before, heard it smack into the solid rock at his back and screech off in murderous ricochet. His mount reared and pawed at the air, plunging in sudden fright. Already, the Coyotero was out of the saddle, on one knee behind his mount, the rifle in his hands, pumping a couple of shots into the rocks. Joel's raking gaze instantly picked out the movement among the boulders as the dry-gulcher tried to back away, knowing that he had failed. Another shot from the hidden gunman, better aimed this time, and he heard a sudden coughing gasp from behind him.

Turning sharply, he saw Cornell lurching in the saddle, an ugly stain forming on his shirt, high up near his right shoulder. The pall of gunsmoke over the rocks gave away the gunman's position again. He had moved slightly, crawled a few yards to his left, hoping to scuttle slantwise over the rocks and back up into the rougher scrub country higher up the slope. Maybe he had his horse waiting up yonder, Joel thought tightly.

Inwardly, he knew that he and the Coyotero would have to nail that killer before they could do anything to help the deputy.

'Get down under cover and stay there,' he yelled harshly to Cornell. 'Try not to move or you'll bleed all the more.'

He did not wait to get a reply or to see whether the other had heard and was obeying him or not. Motioning to the Coyotero, he gestured the other off the trail and up the slope. Rocks and pebbles crunched and slid under his feet as he threw himself forward, keeping his head low, his grip tight on the rifle, painfully aware of the fact that he was almost totally exposed in the harsh glare of sunlight that fell over the lower slopes, almost entirely devoid of cover. Digging in with his toes and heels, he ran forward, dropped behind a protruding rock as a bullet smashed into the top of it, showering him with stinging slivers of stone. He drew in a deep breath, aware that his heart was now pumping madly in his chest. This was how it had often been in the old days with the army, he thought savagely, running down a cunning and elusive enemy. The old ways came back to him now, standing him in good stead. A quick glance over the lip of the rock and he saw the dark shape of the Coyotero glide noiselessly from one rock to another, a bare twenty-five yards away. The other was angling off to one side, would flank the gunman if only Joel could keep the other's head down. The drygulcher must have realized this quite suddenly, for he began firing down the slope with a reckless abandon, striving to keep Joel pinned down.

A quick look around and Joel placed the other behind a small cluster of rocks perhaps two hundred yards up the slope. His gaze took in the narrow gully that angled up from a point less than fifteen yards from where he lay. If he could reach that and get down into it, he would be able to worm his way along it without having to expose himself to the other's fire. He decided to take the chance.

Gripping his rifle in a tight-fisted hold, he threw himself out into the open, darted across the intervening stretch of open ground. The rifle barked again and slugs tore up tiny puffs of powdered rock around his feet as he sprinted up the slope, hurling himself the last two yards, striking the hard ground with a blow that knocked all of the wind out of his lungs, leaving him utterly breathless for several moments, unable to move. Then, off in the sunhazed distance, there came the steady bark of the Coyotero's rifle. Summoning up all of his strength, he thrust himself along the rough bottom of the bare gully, feeling the razor-edged rocks tear at his clothing, lancing into the flesh of his knees and elbows.

At the end, he risked another look. There was no sign of the Coyotero or the hidden gunman. For a long moment there was a deep silence with only the faintly fading echoes of the gunshots dying into the distance. Joel dug in deep with his boots, pushed himself out of the gully, ran for the rocks some thirty yards away. If he could draw the other's fire so that the Coyotero could get in a shot, it could mean the end of the gunman.

He saw the dark figure crouched among the rocks as he threw himself down, saw the other bring his rifle round to cover him. A shot from a little further down the slope hammered into the rocks close beside the other, spoiling the man's aim. Then Joel had inched forward, propped himself up on his elbow and jerked his rifle forward, squeezing the trigger swiftly, the Winchester hammering out four deadly shots.

In the sunlight, he saw the other rear up, come to his knees, then fall back against the rocks as the impact of the lead drove him down on to his haunches. His weapon exploded once, but the slug hit the dirt only a few feet in front of him as he fell forward, the rifle dropping from his grasp. He rolled down the slope in a sprawl of arms and legs, came to rest in a notch between two boulders close to where Joel lay. Slowly, the marshal got to his feet and walked forward, turned the other over with the toe of his boot as the Coyotero came forward. The gunman fell limply on to his back. The man was dead and there was no mistaking the other's features, lips drawn back in a deadly grin even in death. It was Ed Borge, not Sage Venner, as Joel had anticipated.

There would be no more trouble from this one anyway, he reflected, and also no information on where the other two men were headed, by which trail, and why they had split up.

'He's dead,' he said thinly. 'Take a look up there in the rocks. My guess is that he has his mount tied up there and probably the gold. Bring 'em both down to the trail.'

The Coyotero moved off along the slope and Joel made his way swiftly down to where Cornell lay in the shade of a huge upthrusting boulder, nursing his shoulder. His face was blanched, lips tight over his teeth. The wound was a bad one, and the slug was still there, embedded somewhere in the torn flesh. It took Joel only a minute's examination to determine that. The deputy was losing quite a lot of blood and they had to get him to a doctor, otherwise he might go the same way as Monroe. Applying what first aid he could in the circumstances, Joel waited while the Indian returned. He was leading Borge's horse, with the large wheat sack still tied securely to the saddle.

'So he did have his share,' Joel said grimly. 'Reckon it won't do him any good now. We'll take it back with us.'

'The horse is lame,' said the Coyotero in his liquid Spanish. 'That is the reason he stayed to fight.'

Joel nodded. 'Could be he figured if he could drop us from ambush, he would get himself a fresh horse to take him the rest of the way to the border.' He glanced down at Cornell. 'Think you can manage to sit a horse if we get you into the saddle?'

'I reckon so.' The deputy gritted his teeth and moaned deep in his throat as the two men lifted him up into the saddle and the greyness remained on his face as he swayed, leaning forward to grab hold of the reins. His eyes closed for a moment, and it seemed he would topple sideways out of the saddle, but with a supreme effort he forced a tight hold on his buckling consciousness, sucked air into his lungs. 'What happened up there. Did you get Venner?'

'Wasn't Venner,' Joel said sharply. 'It was Ed Borge – and we got him. He's dead now, which is a pity in a way; he might have been able to tell us where the other two are and why they took different trails. Guess we'll have to find them before we know for sure. But first we've got to get you some medical aid and that means a town of some kind.' He glanced at the Coyotero. 'Do you know these parts?' It was, he realized, a forlorn hope. But the other nodded his head slowly in the affirmative.

'There is a mining town about three hours' journey in that direction,' he said, pointing almost due east. 'It might take more than that time with a badly wounded man.'

'Never mind that, it's obviously the only place. They may have a doctor there and it's our only hope. Let's get moving.'

They swung up into the saddles, leading the outlaw's horse behind them. All through the long afternoon, they rode steadily east, the Coyotero leading the way, travelling as fast as they dared, with Cornell swaying in the saddle. At times, it seemed that he was only barely conscious, eyes closing and lidding, head falling forward on to his chest, but somehow, he managed to stay upright in the saddle.

When they finally came down from the rocky ledges and hit the flat ground that ran on towards the dark smudge which was the town, their shadows were lengthening in front of them. They crossed a plank bridge that spanned a narrow creek, rode into the only road that ran through the town; little more than a cluster of perhaps a couple of dozen buildings, slant-roofed erections that seemed to have been thrown up in a hurry along both sides of the road, with no thought to orderliness at all.

A couple of men, seated on the boardwalk, eyed them curiously as they rode in, then got to their feet and came forward.

'This is my deputy,' said Joel quietly, jerking a thumb in Cornell's direction. 'We ran into a dry-gulcher up in the hills and he's been hurt pretty bad. Is there a doctor in this town?'

'Sure, Marshal. I'll get him.' One of the men sprinted along the street as the trio rode forward.

They were almost at the centre of the place when a tall, thin-faced man came out of one of the buildings followed by the man who had met them on the edge of town.

'I'm Doc Cantry,' said the other. 'Get him inside the house and I'll take a look at him.'

Carefully, Cornell was helped from the saddle and carried into the house, stretched out on top of the long table. Cantry carefully slit the blood-soaked shirt with the tip of a knife, peeled it back from the bloody shoulder. When one of the men boiled a can of water over the fire, he fetched his instruments.

'How bad is it, Doc?' Joel asked.

'Too early to say yet. I don't think that slug has gone anywhere near the lung, but it may have splintered the bone and when that happens, there's always the danger of a bone splinter piercing the lung. I'll know in an hour or so after I've probed for that bullet.

He's lost plenty of blood too. How far has he had to travel in that condition?'

'Several hours,' Joel told him. 'We didn't know there was a town near here except that the Coyotero travellin' with us knew this territory.'

'That Indian riding with you?' asked the other, glancing up with an expression of mild surprise on his face.

'That's right. I'm trailing a bunch of outlaws who held up the bank in Benson a little over a week ago. They headed out for the border. We trailed this one through the hills west of here, flushed him out, but not before he'd shot my deputy.'

'And the others?'

'We'll pick up their trail soon,' Joel told him. 'There aren't many men who can hide their trail from a Coyotero.'

'No – I guess you're right.' The other went back to his task, cleaning up the wound. A few moments later, he paused. 'There's nothing you can do here, Marshal. Why don't you rest up for a couple of hours in the other room? You won't be disturbed there and I reckon you'll want to know about your deputy before you pull out of here.'

Joel hesitated. Now that they had finished

one of the men, he wanted to be back on the trail after the others. Yet he knew that to do so would need all of his concentration and both he and the Coyotero needed to be in good condition for the journey.

'All right.' He nodded. 'Thanks. You'll wake me as soon as you've finished. We've a lot of ground to cover.'

'I'll call you,' promised the other. He bent over Cornell as Joel walked wearily to the back room. There was a bed in the corner and, taking off his boots and jacket, he hung his gunbelt over the back of the nearby chair and stretched himself out on the bed. Less than three minutes later, he was sound asleep.

Three hours later, he was wakened by the touch of a hand on his shoulder, came wide awake instantly, eyes jerking open. He swung his legs to the floor and stood up, reaching for the gunbelt.

'How's Cornell?' he asked in a thick voice.

'He'll live if that's what you want to hear,' said the other. 'But that shoulder of his has been smashed pretty badly. It will be some weeks yet before he'll be on his feet and I doubt if he'll ever use that arm properly again. He certainly won't be a deputy again, I'm afraid.'

Joel tightened his lips a little, then nodded. 'I know you're doin' all you can for him, Doc. Is he conscious yet?'

'No. I gave him something to make him sleep. He won't waken for some hours yet, probably not before the morning.'

Joel pulled on his boots, hitched his gunbelt a little higher about his waist. 'No sense in me hangin' around until then,' he said, forcing evenness into his tone. 'I'll be ridin' out in about an hour's time, once I've got some provisions.'

'I wish you luck.' said the other. 'I heard about that hold-up. The Venner gang, wasn't it?'

'That's right. We killed Ed Borge up there in the hills. Venner and Lander are runnin' for the Mexico border.'

Cantry pursed his lips. 'You reckon you'll cut them off before they get there?'

'Maybe not.' He moved towards the door and something in his tone had made the other pause.

Then Cantry said: 'If you don't, then you'll ride over the border after them. That's it, isn't it?'

'That's it.' Joel nodded.

'Can't say I blame you,' went on the other after a momentary pause. 'Too many of them escape the law by operatin' over the border. Pity there's no two-way agreement between our governments to stop this.'

'There may be someday,' Joel said quietly. 'At the moment, we have to operate as we think fit.'

He went out into the street, quiet now with the long shadows of evening lying across it. Collecting provisions, he tied them to the saddle, watched as the Coyotero did likewise. As he swung up into the saddle, Cantry edged forward, throwing a quick, wary glance in the Indian's direction.

'Do you reckon it's wise to trust him with a gun?' he asked in a low voice.

Joel nodded. 'He's already proved that,' he said tightly. 'Besides, those men we're tailin' are carryin' a fortune in gold with them – and gold means absolutely nothin' to a Coyotero. He's better than most men I could have with me.'

Cantry gave a faint grin. 'I get your point, Marshal,' he acknowledged. 'Reckon he has some good points. Just that I never figured I'd see a lawman give a rifle to an Indian.' He shrugged, released his hold on the other's bridle and stepped back. 'I'll take good care of your deputy,' he said, lifting a hand.

'Thanks. If we return this way, we'll look in and see how he's getting on.'

Touching spurs to his mount's flanks, he urged it along the quiet, dusty street of the small town. Already, the night was sweeping in from the east and the first stars were gleaming faintly above the hills.

7

SOUTH OF THE BORDER

Once he was sure that Borge did not intend to swing around and try to box them in against the upthrusting mountain range that ran along the eastern perimeter of the valley, Venner let his thoughts range ahead. He had already been reluctantly forced to give up any idea of going after Borge and killing him. That would have wasted far too much time and taken him well off his trail; besides there was still Lander to take into consideration.

The other was still an inconvenience and already, Venner's fertile mind was scheming ways of getting rid of the other. The trouble was, that Lander was now suspicious. Borge's act in riding off like that, in throwing down a gun on him, had started the train of suspicion in Lander's mind and Venner had seen it growing over the hours and the miles.

They had spent the first night riding

through the bitter cold of the wide mesas, anxious to make as much progress as possible. The second had been in a cluster of high rocks overlooking a broad stage trail. Here, they had not dared to light a fire and during the latter half of the night, Lander had woken him and they had crouched in the bitter cold while a bunch of riders had swept by in the night. Venner had been unable to make out any details of the men, but he had not doubted that it was some posse, warned by Fergus, on the look-out for them. The whole territory from there to the border would be swarming with lawmen and bounty hunters, anxious to capture them and claim a share of the gold. By now, a reward would have been posted for them, a high enough sum to attract more than mere lawmen to their trail.

More than once, he had caught Lander watching him obliquely, had begun to guess what was going through the other's mind.

With the late afternoon sun slanting westwards, dipping from the high arch overhead, they cut away from a narrow ridge trail and moved downslope into a stretch of heavy brush. Except for the faint keening of the wind and the sound of hoofs and saddle leather, the evening was ghostly silent. He shivered a little as he let his thoughts wander. For a moment, he seemed to be hearing voices in the whisper of the wind as it sighed over the gullies and creaked the stiff, dry branches of the mesquite, scratching the tumbleweed over the earth. He rubbed the stubble on his chin, shook himself savagely. The sound of the wind was too much like the last breath of the dying.

Damn, he'd killed men by the score, both during the war and since and he was not the kind of man to believe in ghosts. But it was strange how he should think of them at this time, with the wild, desolate country all about him and only Lander and his own thoughts to keep him company. He tried to rub out the memory of Tollen dying among the rocks; and of Monroe's last bitter curse as they had ridden out of that mountain camp. Where was Monroe now? he wondered, unable to thrust the memory completely from his mind. Dead – still lying back there in that tumble-down shack. Or had the posse, scouring the hills for them, got to him in time? If they had, no doubt he was the one who had put that marshal on their trail.

Anger overcame the faint stirring of

superstitious fear in his mind. Damn Monroe. He ought to have spent a few minutes making sure that the other would not talk.

'You look like a man who's got trouble on his mind,' said Lander suddenly. He eyed Venner warily. 'Still tryin' to figure out a way of gettin' rid of me before we reach the border?'

'You still thinkin' about Borge,' snapped Venner. 'He was nothin' more than a goddamned fool.' He stayed the other with a quick gesture of his right hand. 'By now, he's either dead or headin' back to the jail in Benson. The sooner you realize that we need each other, the better, Lander. We have to put all the distance we can between Fergus and ourselves.'

Something about that struck Lander as funny. He grinned, but there was little mirth in his smile and it never touched his eyes. 'You just put our whole position in a nutshell, Venner. We keep runnin', keep trying to keep some distance between us and Fergus. Damnit all, the man ain't likely to trail us this far. He'll leave it to the other posses.'

'Don't underestimate him. He'll come, maybe even follow us into Mexico.' There was a certainty in Venner's voice that stopped any more questions Lander wanted to put to the other.

They rode over a long, jagged shelf, part of the caprock, still cutting south. The dusk and the breeze formed more shadows, endowing them with human form, stretching their frazzled nerves to fresh limits of apprehension. The ride that day had been a nightmare of hunger and thirst and physical discomfort. Scanning the creeping shadows through tender, smarting eyes, Venner saw the shack just visible among the ridges below them.

He pointed. 'Could be that we'll sleep with a roof over our heads tonight, Lander. That shack there. Probably been deserted for years. Let's take a look-see.'

They topped a low rise, came closer to the shack. It stood lonely and isolated, well away from the trail, evidently thrown up by someone who had no liking for company. Leaning forward in the saddle, Venner squinted down at it, rubbed his knuckles over his eyes for a moment, trying to ease the gritty pain where the sand had penetrated the lids.

'Wait a minute.' His tone was sharp with warning. 'I reckoned I saw smoke from that chimney. The place isn't deserted like I figured.'

'Who the hell would want to live there?' Lander screwed up his lips. ''Way out here, miles from any place.'

'How the hell should I know. Let's ride down there and take a look. Whoever it is, if we watch our step we'll get some grub and shelter for the night, maybe some information about the law in these parts. If the posse has been this way, he's sure to know about it.'

'Could be that he won't like the idea of company.'

Venner grinned wolfishly. 'I ain't particular whether he likes it or not. I've a gun here that says he will.' His fingertips touched the butt of his revolver meaningly. He half drew it, then let it fall back into the holster, raking spurs across his horse's flanks, urging it down the slope.

Night had reached in out of the east when they finally angled down into a shallow slope, less than a quarter of a mile from the shack. The smell of wood smoke drifted to them on the wind, bringing with it the odour of frying food. Lander felt the sharp pain at the edges of his jaw, realized just how hungry he was, how long it had been since they had eaten food properly cooked. He felt a tingling of apprehension too. Whoever lived in that place had no liking for the law, that much seemed certain from the way he lived in this out-of-the-way place, clearly determined to shun the human race.

Soon, they dismounted, went the rest of the way on foot, came out of a thin fringe of stunted timber growth which screened the edge of a shallow saucer of scree-covered land. Parting the bushes, Venner studied the small shack built out of logs hewn from the trees. There was a faint yellow glow of lamplight visible in the window that looked out on to the open ground. The door was shut and there was a thin, faintly-seen coil of smoke lifting from the chimney, hanging in a dull cloud above the rocks which backed the cabin.

'Let's go,' said Lander harshly.

'Not so fast.' Venner caught his arm, held it in a vicelike grip, sliding the Colt from its holster with his other arm. 'We don't know what we're walkin' into yet. We'll scout the place until we're sure. Could be a nester there with a grown-up family.'

'Ain't likely,' Lander muttered. He rubbed his stomach. 'But just so long as I eat. Hell, it seems days since I last had a decent bite.'

Guns out, they made their way silently over a patch of weed, past a small square plot of garden where a few vegetables were growing. They eased their way cautiously to the shack, paused as they came alongside it. Venner bent his head, pressing it close to the wood. He could hear nothing inside, which to him meant there was only one person there. A man who had been on the run like themselves at some time, he guessed; but who had decided to hide out here, to be forgotten by the law, rather than try for the border. Well, every man to his taste.

He motioned Lander forward, around to the other side of the door, lowered his head as he moved past the window, came up to the door and paused, ready to kick it in with his boot. Before he could move, however, a harsh voice at his back snapped: 'Drop those guns and stand away from there!'

Venner stiffened, mumbled an oath under his breath, cursing himself for not having taken the elementary precaution of scouting the place before moving into the open. Of course the other had seen or heard them while they had been some distance away and had left the lamp burning in the hut while he had withdrawn into the brush to the rear. Like fools, they had moved out of cover and were now paying the price of their folly. For a moment, he wondered just where the other was, debating whether he could swing in that direction and get in a shot before the man could press the trigger of the rifle which was almost certainly covering Lander and himself. Then he put the thought out of his mind. Dropping the Colt on to the dirt, he said softly:

'You've got this all wrong, mister. We meant no harm. All we want is some grub and shelter for the night. In the mornin' we'll be on our way. We don't mean you any harm.'

'That's what you say now, with this rifle trained on you.'

Venner heard the sound of footsteps moving stealthily over the weeds, and a moment later, a man moved into his line of vision, a gnarled, weather-beaten man, dressed in loose-fitting clothing, the rifle in his hand covering both of them. No doubt that he was a man who had, at some time or other, taken the wrong trail, got on the wrong side of the law, and was now trying to stay out of sight. Venner prided himself on his ability to read character. The other's eyes gave a lot away.

Swiftly, Venner calculated: 'You anythin' to

do with the law?' He put just the right shade of meaning into the question, saw the other's eyes narrow. There was a look of vague understanding there.

'You those two *hombres* the posse was lookin' for?'

'Could be.' Venner's tone was cautious. 'You figurin' on turnin' us in?' He kept his voice under control. 'Or are you like us, keepin' out of the way of the law?'

The other hesitated, then grinned slyly. 'I've heard a lot of things, even out here,' he said. There was a calculating look on his face. 'They say that some *hombres* managed to raid the bank in Benson, got away with plenty of dinero. Could be you're two of that gang. Word was that three men were headin' for the border. I saw one of the posses go through day before yesterday. Guess you managed to give 'em the slip in the hills.'

'Mind if I lower my hands?' Venner asked.

'Go ahead. But slow. Don't make any funny moves or I'm likely to press this trigger.'

'You couldn't stop both of us,' Venner pointed out. 'Besides, we can pay for food and a bed for the night.'

The other thought that over, then nodded. He lowered the rifle. 'All right. Let's go inside. No sense in standin' out here all night.'

Venner relaxed. The other was still wary, but sooner or later, he felt sure they would be able to catch him off his guard. 'Mind if we take back our guns?'

'No!' Sharp suspicion flared in the man's tone. 'I'll take them until you ride out tomorrow.'

Venner concealed his disappointment. Evidently the other wasn't green. He shrugged. 'Suit yourself. Just so long as we get 'em back before we ride out. From what we've seen there could be trouble lyin' in wait for us and a man feels naked without a gun when the law is lookin' for him clear to the Mexico border.'

'You'll never make it,' said the other, following them inside the shack and closing the door. He still kept a tight grip on the rifle. 'Up here, although I may be some ways off the trails, I see and hear plenty. Not much happens that I don't get to know about sooner or later and I do know there's a big hunt on for you.'

'We've made it so far and I reckon we can slip through any lawmen who try to stand between us and the border,' Venner said quietly. He glanced at the stove, went over to it, forcing casualness into his actions. Whatever happened, now was not the time to make any rash moves. He had seen the shine of greed that had shown in the other's eyes when he had recognized them for two of the outlaws who had held up the Benson bank. The other was, even now, scheming how to get his hands on some of that gold. Venner intended to play along with this until the other gave him the chance of grabbing that rifle.

'Frijoles.' Venner stared down into the pan on the stove. The smell of the food assailed him afresh. 'Lander. Guess we struck it right this time. Better put some more on.'

The other nodded. 'There's corn meal in the corner too. Want me to mix us some corn bread?'

'Sure. Coffee too.' Venner seated himself in the chair in one corner of the room, making himself at ease, outwardly resting, but from beneath lowered lids, watching the thin-faced man closely. 'Tomorrow we'll buy some grub from you to see us over the rest of the journey.'

'You sure that you got money to pay?' There was a sharp look in the other's beady glance. 'Could be that you're just a couple of saddle bums drifting through.'

'Guess that's a risk you'll just have to take,' said Venner softly. 'Unless you want one of us to go back to our horses and bring up some of the gold just to convince you.'

He saw the other's tongue work around his lips greedily. For a moment, he thought the other was on the point of agreeing, then he shook his head. 'I'll take the chance,' he said sharply.

Venner shrugged. He had hoped inwardly that the other would have fallen for that. If he had been able to go alone, he would have got the rifle from the scabbard and the next time, he would not have made the same mistake as before. Clearly, this possibility had occurred to the other. He wasn't going to fall for anything like that.

With a fresh alertness, the man said: 'Where are your horses right now?'

'Back along the trail a piece,' Lander said, looking up from the stove. 'You reckon they'll be safe enough there? Wouldn't like anybody to come along and find 'em during the night.'

The man's grin disappeared at that thought, then he relaxed. 'Don't reckon there'll be anybody around these parts. We're well off the trail. That's why I chose this position in the first place.'

Lander brought the frijoles to the table. While they ate ravenously, the man watched them from the corner. Not until they had finished, washing the food down with the hot coffee, did he speak. 'There are a couple of bunks in the other room.'

'You not wantin' one of 'em?' Venner asked, putting surprise into his voice.

The other shook his head. 'I get plenty of rest up here with nothin' to disturb me. Just take 'em both. Won't hurt me to stay awake through the night.'

Venner guessed what was on the other's mind, saw that Lander suspected it too, but before the other could say anything in protest, he had got to his feet, gripping Lander's arm. 'Guess we'll accept your offer, friend,' he murmured. 'We're both pretty tired after bein' on the trail for so long. But if you got any plans of runnin' out on us and warnin' the law, better forget them.' The note of menace in his tone did not pass unnoticed by the other.

'I got no likin' for the law, mister,' he said. 'Such a thing never entered my mind.'

'Sure it didn't,' murmured Venner. Turning, he went through the low door into the other room, motioning to Lander to follow him.

Once inside, the other swung sharply on him. 'What the hell did you do that for? Don't you realize that the minute we're asleep he'll scout around for the horses and find that gold?'

'Sure, he will,' Venner nodded, keeping his voice low. 'That's what I want him to do. As soon as he slips out of the cabin, we leave too. Only we know just where the horses are and we can reach 'em before he gets there. Once I get that rifle in my hands, I'll pay him for the food with a bullet.'

Lander squinted hard at him for a moment, then nodded. He moved across the room, picked one of the low iron bunks and stretched himself out on it, hands clasped at the back of his neck.

Starke could almost smell the gold. In the other room of the cabin, he sat at the low table, staring into the lamp-glow, the little voice in his brain whispering softly, insistently: *Get it all for yourself. You have the rifle. Wait until they're asleep and then slip out, find the horses, spook one of them and take the other.*

He had heard the horses downgrade a little way before the two men had made such a racket pushing through the brush on the far edge of the plateau. He felt sure he could locate the animals within minutes and that the gold these two men had stolen would be tied to the saddles of their mounts. A tight eagerness took hold of him. He got slowly to his feet, moved over to the door and pressed his ear tight against it, listening intently. He could hear nothing from inside the room. Both men had looked tired when they had arrived. He guessed they had ridden non-stop for two or three days. With a posse close on their heels, they would not pause long for sleep during the night, but would push both their horses and themselves to the utmost limit. He doubted if they would be able to resist sleep for long once they stretched themselves out on those bunks.

He waited for a further ten minutes, then gently lifted the latch and thrust the door open a couple of inches. The room beyond was in darkness, but sufficient of the yellow light from the lamp penetrated the room for him to be able to make out the two men stretched out on the bunks. Both were snoring loudly, making no move. Finally satisfied, he closed the door, picked up the rifle from the corner, left the lamp still burning on the table, opened the outer door and moved cautiously out into the night.

The faint glimmer of starshine lay over the swaying tops of the trees and there was only the keening murmur of the wind rustling through the mesquite and weeds breaking the stillness. He strode rapidly over the open patch of ground, plunged into the trees on the far side. Pausing for just a moment, he looked back towards the shack. No movement of any kind there. A tight-lipped grin twisted his lips as he turned back and moved deeper into the dark shadow of the trees.

He found the trail where the two men had pushed their way through the brush, followed it cautiously in the darkness. Thorns scratched the back of his hands and raked over his face, but he scarcely noticed them. His brain was afire with but a single thought. If those two were part of that gang which had robbed the Benson bank, then there would be the best part of thirty thousand dollars' worth of gold and banknotes in those saddle-bags.

The trail petered out as he reached the more open ground. Tensely, he pushed his gaze through the darkness, trying to pick out the shapes of the horses. He saw nothing, moved around in a wide circle, eyes alert. Ten minutes later, he paused near a clump of trees, frustrated. Damn it all, they had to be somewhere close by. It wasn't likely that those men had travelled so far on foot after spotting the shack. Besides, he had heard them plainly, riding along the trail.

Drawing air down into his lungs, he moved forward again. Coming out on to a low, flat rock, he paused. A sound off to his left jarred the stillness, shattering the silence like crystal. He listened, heard it repeated. The sound of an iron-shod hoof on solid rock. His grin returned, and he went forward more quickly now.

Pushing through a tumble of rocks, he spotted the two horses standing hipshot less than ten yards away, in a narrow causey among the rocks. He must have moved within twenty yards of them when he had first circled around in this direction and missed seeing them altogether.

Going down into the depression, he came up to the mounts. They shied away from him as he approached them, straining at the leather which held them to a stump jutting out of the earth. Clucking softly, he quietened them, patted the nearest on the neck.

'Steady boy,' he murmured. 'Nothing's goin' to happen to you.' Reaching up, he felt for the saddle-bag, found it, explored the wheat sack with his fingers. There was no doubting the feel of gold, even through the cloth. A feeling of exultation went through him and he sucked in a sharp breath. Once he got the other sack, he would tie it to the saddle, spook the other horse and ride out of here. If the posse caught up with those two at the shack, it was just too bad.

Moving his hand, his fingers caught the scabbard fastened to the saddle. A second later, the realization came to him that the scabbard was empty, yet neither of those men had been carrying a rifle when he had surprised them at the shack. Even as the shock of the discovery flashed a warning to his brain, there was a sudden sound at his back. Whirling swiftly, his hand striking for the rifle which he had laid on the ground beside him, he knew instinctively that it was too late. He had walked right into a trap set by those men. Somehow they had tricked him, had left the shack once he had moved into the trees and, knowing exactly where to go, they had taken their rifles and lain in wait for him.

His fingers touched the butt of the rifle at

the same moment that the blue-crimson flash came out of the darkness of the rocks less than ten feet away. He was only briefly aware of the roar of the weapon when the lead struck him in the soft parts, driving him back against the horse.

Venner walked forward slowly, prodded the still form over on to its back with his foot, then lowered the Winchester. 'He's dead,' he said tonelessly. 'Never knew what hit him.'

'What do we do now?' queried Lander, moving out of the shadows.

Venner gave a sharp laugh. 'Seein' as he was so glad to offer us the hospitality of the shack for the night, I reckon we're entitled to it.'

'We'll have to bury him first.'

'Like hell we will,' Venner exploded. 'We'll leave him for the coyotes. He'd have taken the gold and ridden out, leavin' us stranded here. Maybe even come back to the shack and put a bullet into us while we were asleep. Why waste time and energy on a critter like that?'

Lander made to reply, then bit the words down. There was no sense in trying to argue with Venner when he had made up his mind and there was no doubt of the truth of what he said.

Ten minutes later, they led their horses over the open ground to the shack, tied them to a rail at the back and went inside.

They pulled out early the next morning after eating their fill of the grub in the shack, filling their pouches with enough to last them all the way to the border. The going was tough now, really tough. These were the Badlands. Vast stretches of arid ground from which the tall buttes lifted in a maze of stark beauty. Here there were no trails at all, no landmarks to guide them through this crazy wilderness carved by Nature on such a vast scale that the mind seemed utterly dwarfed by it all, unable to take it all in. Despite this, Venner seemed to know exactly where to go and Lander rode along silently. He had hardly spoken a dozen words since they had killed that man and several times he threw a worried, apprehensive look at Venner. He saw nothing but disaster ahead of them now. It had seemed to start off all right with everything running smoothly after they had robbed the bank and ridden out of Benson. Each event seemed to fit into place without any trouble. But it had all started to go sour on them once they had left that shack in the hills. Maybe it would have been better if they had waited up there for a few more days. It had scared Lander to see the crazy look which had crossed Venner's face when Borge had pulled that gun on him and ridden out. Now he was alone with Venner and he felt a little more scared than ever. Just look at the way in which they had been whittled down. Tollen shot by Venner, Monroe left back there in that shack to die. Borge gone, and now Lander felt sure the other was dead. They had started out to ride into Benson as five highly dangerous men and as a bunch they had made a formidable crew.

With an effort he pushed the thought out of his mind. They were still free, still had the gold and the border was not too many miles ahead. It was no use thinking of what might have happened if they had only made different decisions somewhere along the line. They were tempting the fates, that was all.

All of that day, they rode south, through the blistering heat of the sun, the glaring light reflected from the rocks and sand striking at them in dizzying waves until they were swaying uncontrollably in their saddles. Their mounts, too, were in a bad way, moving slowly now. The caustic alkali in the sand had burned their feet, making them raw and tender and even Venner was a little doubtful as to how much further they would be able to carry them.

By nightfall they came out into a series of wide canyons that slashed the ground with deep scars. Riding along the bottom of one of them, with the rocks towering high over them, they felt the coolness of the night wind in their faces, knew they were approaching the hills which they had seen around noon, looming high on the southern horizon. Venner had been certain that the border lay just to the south of the range and now they pushed their mounts forward as fast as they dared.

'Do we camp for the night or keep on riding?' Lander asked, turning slightly in the saddle. He felt bone-weary and the heat of the day had sucked all of the moisture out of him.

Venner threw a quick look along the wide canyon, out to the point where it opened out on to a stretch of ground that began to rise up towards the towering crests of the mountains. 'We'll ride on through the night,' he decided. 'Another few hours should do it. Once we're over the border they won't be able to touch us.' He himself felt uncertain about that, but he had the feeling that once they reached San Antonio, he would have a much better chance of standing off Fergus if he did decide to ride after them. The marshal would have no jurisdiction in Mexico and they would be on level terms then.

They stayed with the main trail upwards and it took them presently to one of the many small, narrow stretches of lush country that creased over the low foothills. Running across it, the main trail continued upward but at this point, Venner jerked a hand to his right and they swung off the trail, into the timber that grew here, old first growth pine, massive at the butt, growing smooth and slender towards the thick umbrella of branches and leaves that grew overhead.

Venner knew nothing about this country, yet he felt no concern. It was no different from that which they had ridden through in the past and so long as they ran into nobody for the next twenty or thirty miles, he would be quite content. Considering this, he rode steadily with Lander following close behind. Beyond the timber, he knew the terrain would be more open and they would be able to hold to the higher ridges as much as possible before crossing the range and heading down towards Mexico.

8

SAN ANTONIO

Wheel tracks marked the trail that led into San Antonio, cutting deep into the ground. Over the years, the tracks had deepened until now they formed wide ruts, inches deep with water whenever the rains came, but now dried and caked hard by the fierce heat of the Mexican sun. Joel and the Coyotero had followed the trail for almost three hours now, ever since an early dawn had brightened the eastern horizon and they had finished a quick breakfast before starting on the last lap of the trail. They had seen no sign of Venner and Lander for almost three days, but from the posses which they had encountered during the long ride south, it had become increasingly obvious that the others were still ahead of them, that they had not backtracked anywhere along the trail, and by now, were most likely here in San Antonio, living off their ill-gotten gains.

Joel felt the tightness in him rise to a fresh peak of intensity. It had been growing stronger and more difficult for him to control over the miles and the days and now it was the one force that drove him on, the desire to see Venner standing in front of his guns.

He glanced about him as he rode, seeing the vast, empty sweep of the plains, golden in the sunlight, yellow hummocks of ground sweeping away in all directions to lose themselves in the distance. There were knots of grazing cattle here and there and gaily-dressed men herding them, lean, dark-skinned men with dark, liquid eyes that watched them curiously as they rode past.

Half an hour later, the Coyotero pointed off into the sun-hazed distance. 'San Antonio,' he said tonelessly. 'Another hour.'

Joel nodded, narrowed his eyes. The town lay directly ahead of them, was the only place of any size for many miles and the most likely place towards which the two outlaws would ride.

An hour later, they rode into the town. Joel had the feel of eyes on him from both sides, but he shrugged it off. He had taken the precaution of removing the badge from his shirt. The people here had no love for the lawmen from over the border and he felt sure he could expect little or no help from the authorities. What he had to do, he must do himself.

They reined their mounts in front of the small cantina. Here the street was wide and lazy, flanked by the low-roofed adobes. All around them was the usual collection of goats and hounds.

Turning to the Coyotero, Joel said: 'You scout around. See if you can raise a smell of them. They're here someplace, I'm sure of that.'

The other nodded, gestured towards the rifle in its scabbard, but Joel shook his head. 'No, if you find them, get back to me here and let me know. I don't want them shot down until I've had a chance to talk to them.'

'Two bullets and it will all be over,' said the other in Spanish.

'No,' Joel repeated. 'There are some questions I want to ask them. It isn't goin' to be as easy and as quick as that for them.'

He knew that neither Venner or Lander would recognize the other, and that the Coyotero had not been boasting when he had implied that he would shoot down the two men with so little trouble.

The other stared down at him impassively for a long moment, saw the look of decision on the marshal's face, nodded again, swung his horse and walked it slowly along the dusty street. Dismounting, Joel went inside the small cantina. It was cool there, out of the heat and light of the sun and he found himself a table where he could see the door and also watch the street through the window nearby.

The Mexican woman who served him spoke only Spanish but he knew enough to make himself understood. When she had brought him his food and the chilled wine, he asked: 'Do you know if two strangers have ridden into town any time in the last day or so, *señora?*'

She shook her head quickly, too quickly, her gaze sliding away from his. He knew she was lying, that she was probably afraid and it came to him that Venner had probably passed the word around most of the places in town and he could expect to get no information from them.

'Are you sure?'

'*Sí*, I am sure. What kind of men are you looking for?'

'Two killers.' Joel said grimly. 'They robbed a bank over the border, shot some men. They rode here thinking they would escape.'

The woman gave him a swift, worried look. 'There has been no one here.'

'I understand.' He nodded, went back to the food. He wondered how the Coyotero would get on, hunting for the two men. If anybody could find them in this place, he could. He was content for the moment to let things go on as they were. His mind and body were weary from the long ride south from Benson and he knew that more than anything now, he needed sleep.

'Have you got a room here where I could stay for the night?' he asked, going over to the low counter.

The woman hesitated, looked quickly about her, then nodded. 'Through there,' she said, pointing to the back of the counter.

'I'm much obliged.' He stepped through into the small room at the rear of the building. There was little furniture there and the floor was of baked earth, but there was a low bunk in one corner and the sheets on it looked cool and inviting.

Still unsure of the woman, knowing that she might have been scared enough by Venner to warn the other of his presence there, he placed his gun under the pillow, one hand around it, before falling asleep.

When he woke, there was a grey light filtering into the room through the small square window set in the wall. He swung his legs to the floor, moved over to it and glanced out. It was grey dawn outside and the town seemed quiet. The sound of a solitary rider cut through the stillness, then the steady abrasion of the other's travel faded and the stillness returned. It was almost sunrise. He had slept through the afternoon and all night without intending to.

He found some water in an earthenware pitcher and poured it into a washbowl. The previous afternoon he had been so tired he had fallen asleep with the dust of the trail still on him. Bending, he washed his face, felt the mask of trail dust crack as the water touched it. Tough as his skin was, it had been scorched by the sun.

He tarried in his room until he heard movement through the wall, then went out. The Mexican woman was bent over the stove, frying frijoles and meat. After he had eaten, he went out into the street. The sun was still somewhere below the horizon, but there was a growing heat in the air and in the distance, to the west of the town, the tall crests of the hills were touched with a pale rose light. He made a slow swing of the centre of the town, then picked up his mount and walked it over to the livery stable.

Leading his horse into one of the stalls at the rear, he was on the point of moving out again when a sudden movement and a quiet voice halted him. The Coyotero came out of the dim shadows.

'Did you find anything?'

'They rode into San Antonio the day before yesterday. No doubt that they are the two men you're looking for.'

'Where are they now?'

'One of them is staying at the hotel along the street. The second man was there, but he pulled out last night.'

Joel knit his brows in puzzled thought. Why should the two of them split up now, when they had reached San Antonio? Had it happened somewhere along the trail, he could have understood it. But surely Venner did not intend to gun down Lander here? Although the law of the United States could not touch him officially, they would now be under the jurisdiction of Mexican law and there would be the same death penalty for murder here as across the border to the north.

'What do you want me to do now?' queried the other. He gestured with his rifle significantly, but Joel shook his head. 'I'll take care of this,' he said. 'I want you to watch the street in case that other man comes back.'

The other nodded, stepped silently back into the shadows out of sight. Leaving the stables, Joel made his way along the street towards the hotel.

Lander sat on the edge of the bed, goggling up at Joel as if he were seeing a ghost. He switched his gaze jerkily to the gunbelt lying close by on the low table and the marshal, catching the direction of the other's gaze, said quietly: 'Go on, Lander. Just make a try for it. That's what I'm waitin' for you to do. I'll give you more of a chance than you gave Tollen, or those men you shot down in your raids along the frontier.'

'I never shot Tollen,' said the other harshly. His lips were quivering slackly as he jerked the words out. 'It was Venner. I swear it.'

'You were in all this with him,' went on the other remorselessly. 'You rode with him and in my eyes that make you just as guilty as he is.'

'But I had to ride with him. Don't you see that? Goddamnit, there was nothin' I could do. He was just lookin' for the excuse to kill me and take my share of the gold.'

'Then why didn't he? How come he allowed you to get to San Antonio without drawin' on you and snatchin' your share? And what happened to Ed Borge? How was it that he rode off and left you along the trail? I want some questions answered, Lander, and I reckon now's as good a time as any.' He drew the Colt slowly from its holster, clicked the hammer back with his thumb. It was only a slight sound in the stillness of the room, but the beads of sweat popped out on the other's forehead and he put out both hands as though in an attempt to fend off something terrible.

'Don't shoot, Fergus. I'll talk. I'll tell you anythin' you want to know.'

'That's better,' Joel seated himself in the chair near the door, his gun not wavering an inch as he kept it levelled on the other's chest. He could see the fear at the back of the other's eyes, could almost smell it from him.

'It was Sage who planned the robbery, like he did all the others. He said that if we was to split up, ride into Benson after dark from different directions and put up in different places, not meetin' until it was time to take the bank, nobody would suspect there was anythin' wrong and we'd be out of the town with the money before anybody realized what was happenin'.'

'And that's how it happened,' put in Joel grimly.

'Sure. We got the money and rode out. But we bumped into you on the outskirts of town and it was then that Monroe got it in the shoulder.'

'And Tollen? How did he come to be shot. That Venner as well?'

'Yeah,' blurted the other. He rubbed the back of his hand over his forehead, his gaze fixed on the round black hole in the gun barrel that was staring him in the face. 'I don't know exactly what happened. I was in the shack when Tollen and Venner went out to take a look around. Venner had been sayin' that we ought to hide out there for a few more days just in case you had men watchin' the trail down from the hills, but Tollen wanted to have his share of the gold and ride out – said he was prepared to take his chances with any posse he might meet on the way. Then we heard the shots and ran out to find that Tollen was dead. Venner said

233

that he'd been held up at gunpoint and forced to dig up the gold out of the cache. He'd managed to knock the gun out of Tollen's hand and shoot him down. That was when we left Monroe in the shack and headed here.'

'That left three of you,' said Joel grimly. 'Where did Ed Borge leave you?'

'Just after we'd crossed the desert,' babbled the other swiftly, the words tumbling from his shaking lips in a torrent. 'He pulled a gun on Venner, said that he was ridin' out and if the other tried to head after him, he'd shoot him out of the saddle. Reckon he must've meant it too because Venner was mad, but he never went after him.'

Joel nodded. 'It might interest you to know that Borge is dead. He decided to shoot it out with us when his horse went lame.'

'I guessed that,' nodded the other dully. 'I told Venner that was what must have happened.'

'And where is Venner now?'

'I don't know. He left yesterday, pulled out. Could be he's ridin' on. He may have figured you'd follow us here, even across the border.'

'But you don't know where he is?' Joel lifted his brows, staring hard at the other.

'No. He never told me and–'

'I think you're lyin'.' Joel's voice was soft, almost gentle. 'I think you know exactly where he is at this very minute. I think you were both so scared that I might trail you here that you decided you'd better make some plan to take me by surprise, so it was decided that you'd stay here where it would be easy to find you, while Venner hid himself somewhere in town, ready to drop me.'

'No, I swear that isn't true. He–'

'Save your breath,' Joel said harshly. 'There's one way of findin' out whether you're lyin' to me or not.' He got to his feet, moved over to the other. Lander shrank away from him, pressing himself back against the wall behind the bed, eyes wide, still fixed on the gun which moved threateningly towards him.

'What are you goin' to do? You can't shoot me down in cold blood! You can't kill an unarmed man. Besides, the noise of a shot would warn the rest of the hotel and you've got no authority here.' He tried to force conviction into his voice.

'I don't aim to kill you,' Joel said. He saw the expression of relief that flitted over the other's features. 'Now get on your feet. You and I are goin' to take a little walk.'

Lander licked his lips nervously. His gaze flicked towards the door. 'Where are we going?'

'You and I are going to take a little walk along the street. I've got the feeling that Venner is close by, that he's watching this place, maybe saw me come into the hotel. By now, there could he a rifle lined up on the entrance outside, ready to drop me the minute I step through the door on to the street.'

He caught the quick look on Lander's face, knew that this was close to the truth. Reaching out, he gripped the other's arm, hauled him off the bed, on to his feet. 'I reckon we're of similar build, you and I. With my hat on your head, you could easily pass for me.'

'You're not going to send me out there in the street,' gasped the other. He squirmed desperately, trying to break free of the lawman's grip, lips drawn back across his teeth.

'What's the matter, Lander? You ain't scared, are you? You said yourself that Venner is away, that you don't know where he is.'

'That's true, but—' The other broke off with a bleat of pain as Joel twisted his arm viciously. Thrusting him forward, he forced the other in front of him, out of the room, along the corridor and down the narrow stairs. The lobby was empty when they entered. Lander renewed his struggles as Joel thrust him towards the door. Jabbing the muzzle of his Colt hard into the small of the other's back, Joel cut off his protests. 'If Venner ain't out there you got nothin' to worry about,' he snapped.

Thrusting his Colt back into its holster, he drew his hat from his head, clamped it on to the other's head, released his hold on the man's arm, and drew the Colt again. 'Now walk out of that door,' he said harshly. His voice was sharp with warning. 'You've got ten seconds.'

Lander turned, stared at him. Hate glared out of his eyes, and his lips kept twisting without any sounds coming out. For a moment, he seemed on the point of launching himself at Joel, regardless of the gun held on him. Then, abruptly, he turned, moved towards the door, pausing hesitantly in the entrance. He leaned forward a little, threw a quick, apprehensive glance along the grey-lit street in both directions.

'Get,' said Joel tightly. He jabbed the other again in the back, heard the gasp of pain that escaped unbidden from the gunman's lips. Then Lander had thrown himself out of the door, was running along the street, yelling at the top of his voice: 'For God's sake, don't shoot, Venner. It's me – Lander.'

He ran five steps before anything happened. Then the silence was split by the vicious crack of a rifle. Lander staggered at the same moment that Joel reached the door, pressing himself in against the upright.

In the middle of the street, Lander had halted as though he had been punched in the stomach by an invisible fist. Then, slowly, he turned, staring back at Joel, a look of stunned surprise on his face. A long sigh came out of him and his knees bent under him as though unable to bear his weight. Sagging, he fell to the dirt, arms and legs slumping loosely under him.

Swiftly, Joel ran his gaze along the buildings on the far side of the street. He saw the faint puff of gunsmoke almost at once, dissipating rapidly but still visible and unmistakable. A second later, he saw the dark shadow that ran along the flat roof of one of the adobe buildings little more than a hundred yards along the street.

Two men ran from one of the buildings a few yards away, bent over the dying man in the street. Moving forward, Joel approached them. One of the men looked up. He let his gaze rest on the Colt at Joel's hip, then said harshly: 'Did you see the shooting, *señor?*'

Joel nodded. Then pointed. 'There was a man on the roof of that building. He used a rifle. I was just coming out of the hotel.'

'Do you know this man?'

Joel hesitated, then nodded. 'His name is Lander. He's wanted for bank robbery and murder north of the border.'

The man's eyes narrowed for a moment, then he said tightly: 'And you have an idea who might have shot him?'

'Yes. His partner, a man named Sage Venner. They rode into San Antonio two days ago.'

'How do you know this, *señor?*' There was a look of suspicion on the Mexican's face.

Joel decided that his only hope now lay in making a clean breast of everything. Taking the badge from his pocket, he showed it to the other. 'I'm Marshal Fergus from Benson,' he explained. 'I've been trailin' these two men for two weeks now.'

'I see.' The suspicion vanished almost

completely, although the other's tone was still guarded. 'You realize, of course, that you have no powers here in Mexico.'

'I understand that, but–'

'But you still have your job to do.' The other smiled a little. 'I, too, am a lawman here, Marshal. If there is any help I can give you, please ask for it.'

For a moment, Joel stared at the other in faint surprise. This was the last thing in the world he had expected. 'I'm much obliged,' he said finally. 'I hope you'll understand if I say this is a very personal matter. That robbery took place in my town and I want to be the one to bring Venner in, alive or dead.'

'Of course. So long as this is something confined to the two of you, I–' The other broke off sharply as a fresh sound reached them from along the street.

Joel swung swiftly. In the first red rays of the rising sun, he spotted the rider spurring his mount out of town, lifting the grey dust behind him.

The moment he had pulled the trigger, Venner had realized that the man running along the street was not Fergus. He had reached his position on the adobe roof just in time to see the marshal make his way into

240

the hotel and had settled down to wait, knowing that if Lander played his part properly they would nail the other without any trouble and the one threat to their existence would have been removed. Somehow, the other had guessed their plan and had forced Lander to wear his hat, to move out into the street ahead of him, to catch the bullet intended for him.

Now, as he rode hell for leather out of the town, he knew that he had overplayed his hand. Fergus would be on his trail within minutes and he could not possibly hope to outrun the other. As he rode, he pushed his gaze ahead of him, searching the terrain, looking for a spot where he could set up an ambush for the other.

He was desperately afraid now and his fear drove all caution from his mind. This was to be the showdown and it came to him then in a flash of certainty that only one of them was going to get up and walk away from this.

A mile further on and he swung sharply in the saddle, watching for the tell-tale cloud of dust that would give him warning of the lawman's pursuit. He spotted it a little while later, far down along the trail, but coming up fast.

It was all he needed. Digging rowels into his horse's flanks, he urged it forward at a cruel pace. He had no thought for his mount now. It would not have to carry him far, but it was essential that he should reach a spot where he would hold the initiative.

The ground up ahead looked fairly open and he cursed harshly under his breath, eyes searching for a suitable spot. Then, off to the right of the trail, he spotted the low, irregular rise of ground, dotted with a handful of trees and tangled brush. It was the only place for miles where there was any cover to be had and it held a commanding view over the surrounding countryside. Jerking savagely on the reins, pulling the horse around so that he almost unseated himself, he raced his mount towards it. Dropping from the saddle on the run, grabbing up the Winchester as he hit the dirt, he let the horse run on, diving for the cover of the vegetation which grew profusely around the bases of the trees.

He lay winded for several moments, then forced himself to move as he picked up the faint drum of hoofbeats in the distance, coming closer rapidly. Heaving himself forward on arms and knees, he lay flat on his stomach, breathing heavily, peering through the brush at the oncoming rider. A vicious grin split his features.

This time, he told himself, there was going to be no mistake. There was scarcely an inch of cover out there and with the Winchester, he could hit the other before he got within two hundred yards of the knoll. Things could scarcely have been better as far as he was concerned. Taking his time, he drew a bead on the approaching rider, his finger resting lightly on the trigger, the butt of the rifle held tightly into his shoulder, his cheek resting against the polished wood.

Narrowing his eyes against the glare of the sun, now lifting clear of the horizon, shining directly into his eyes, Joel slowed his mount abruptly. In the distance, he could just make out the long streamer of grey dust lifted by the running horse, but he had the feeling that there was no one in the saddle. The knoll, just off to his right, seemed far too tempting a spot for Venner to have passed up in his headlong flight. The other would have known instinctively that he could only run so far, that sooner or later he would be forced to hole up and fight; and in country he did not know, he could not be sure of finding any cover out there in the wilderness that stretched away to the east with the trail curving over it like a pale grey scar in the brightening sunlight.

No, the chances were that he had chosen the first place that offered him cover and had let his horse go on, hoping to throw Joel off the scent. It was one of the oldest tricks in the book.

Leaning forward, he slid the Winchester from the scabbard, checked that it was loaded, then held it lightly in his right hand, as he walked his mount forward. If Venner was hidden in that thick growth on top of the knoll, there was no point in hurrying things. He let his gaze wander over the position, taking in every detail. There was little cover in the open ground surrounding the knoll, he noticed, the ground flat and open, with only a narrow gully, scarcely two feet deep at its greatest depth, angling across it, some hundred and fifty yards from the trees. If he could get into that he might stand a chance, but it was not going to be easy and the odds were that Venner still possessed that rifle he had used to kill Lander, and he would be able to hit him easily from that range.

Momentarily, his eyes caught a vague movement in the brush. He raised the

Winchester, sighted it on the spot and although he knew himself to be at the utmost limit of the weapon's range, he squeezed off a couple of shots, felt the gun kick against his wrist. The return fire was almost immediate. The bullet went wide of him, but the warning that Venner was there, ready and waiting for him, was enough. He studied the terrain thoughtfully. He was slightly lower than Venner's position and somehow, he had to make it to that shallow gully.

Much of the ground between it and him was of open rock. Sliding from the saddle, he looped the reins over his horse's neck, moved off to one side, keeping low, the rifle trailing in his right hand. Another shot kicked up dust some twenty yards off. Evidently the other was having difficulty in getting the range. That gave Joel heart. It still meant that he was going to have to risk his life getting to that gully, but if he could draw the other's fire until he was forced to reload the rifle, he might have his chance.

Deliberately, he moved closer. Two more shots. Now he probably had only the one left. There was just the chance that the other would reload now, to be on the safe side, but Joel did not consider this likely. The other could never be sure when he would make a run for that gully. Dropping to his knees, he crawled forward, was less than twenty yards from the edge of the gully when the sixth shot came. It shattered a rock only ten feet in front of him, splinters kicking back and striking him on the face in a stinging shower. For a moment, the pain made him pause. Then, getting to his feet, he thrust himself forward with all the strength in his legs, bobbing and weaving from side to side to present a more difficult target. His heart was in his mouth every foot of the way, not knowing when the next shot might come, whether he had made a mistake or not. He hurled himself forward the last three feet, dropped on to hands and knees among the loose rocks and shale that lined the bottom of the gully, stretched himself out flat.

Three seconds later, four shots hammered into the stillness and he heard the low-pitched hum of the slugs as they burned through the air over his prone body, smashing into the rocks only feet away. He aimed quickly at the spot from where the muzzle fire had lanced. Now be ready for him, he thought tensely. He crawled along behind the cover of the low rocks which bordered the gully. It was less than fifteen yards long, but it gave him some room in which to manoeuvre in spite of the fact that he was now pinned down by the gunman on the knoll. Lifting his head slowly, he tried to make out the shape of the other, but be could no longer see it and he had no intention of wasting any more ammunition firing at shadows.

He settled down to wait. Now, he thought grimly, we shall see just how good he is, whether or not the silence and the waiting is going to tell on his nerves. Inwardly, he felt sure that Venner had less true patience than he knew. His elbows raised him enough to be able to see through a small gap in between a couple of the rocks. He let his gaze rove over the length and breadth of the knoll, what he could see of it. Time passed slowly, each minute dragging itself out into an individual eternity. The heat increased. The rocks under his body grew hot, burning him through his clothing. He felt the sweat come out of every pore, soak into his garments.

Forcing himself to ignore the discomfort, he narrowed his eyes to mere slits. Maybe once the waiting has got on his nerves a little, he'll be ready to give himself up, Joel thought grimly. Almost at once, his logical mind rejected the notion. Venner had killed too many men, had been implicated in their murders by Lander. He would know this by now, would know that if he was taken a prisoner, there would inevitably be a noose waiting for him. He would prefer to shoot it out here.

A sudden yell from the knoll jerked his head round. Venner had evidently moved his position.

'You still out there, Fergus?'

Joel watched the brush, tried to pinpoint the origin of the voice. 'I'm still here, Venner. What's on your mind?'

'Look, Marshal. Reckon your pay ain't much doin' that job. What say we make a deal, you and me?'

'What sort of a deal do you want to make, Venner?'

'There's plenty of gold there for the two of us. You could live a life of luxury here. Why go back to fifty dollars a month in Benson? Ain't nothing there for you, riskin' your life every day for a pittance. You could have everythin' you want here.'

'Sounds interestin',' Joel called back. 'And supposin' I was to say yes. I'd stand up and get a bullet in my back for my trouble. You're not foolin' me, Venner. Come out of there with your hands lifted and I'll personally see that you get a fair trial.'

There was a harsh laugh from the other. 'I'm damned sure you will. A quick drop on the end of a rope. You're a fool, Marshal. Turnin' down my offer. Because that means I've got to kill you. A few hours out there in this sun and the top of your head will be frying. You'll not know what's happening. I've seen it all before, seen men come in after a few hours in the desert. Ain't no cover for you there, but I've got all the shade I need here.'

'We'll see who cracks first, Venner.' Joel settled back on the sun-scorched rocks. The heat was oppressive and he knew that the other had hit on the one fundamental weakness of his position. There was no protection from the full fiery heat of the sun out there in the gully.

Throughout the next two hours, there was no sound from the knoll. Joel kept his eyes on it, occasionally shifting his body into a fresh position as the clawing fingers of cramp thrust themselves through his limbs. He smoked a few cigarettes to pass the time, pulled the brim of his hat down over his forehead.

A little after three o'clock, with the sun

slowly dipping from its zenith and the heat head lifted to its maximum piled-up intensity, he caught the sudden movement in the brush. Narrowing his gaze, he saw Venner crawl over a stretch of open ground, slither out of sight again, behind one of the trees. Thinning his lips back across his teeth, Joel shifted the rifle slightly, watching the spot where the other had vanished. When the other did not appear on the other side, he moved to the very end of the gully. A second later, the other betrayed his keyed-up nervousness by firing recklessly among the rocks that stretched along the edge of the gully.

For a moment, Joel was taken by surprise at the other's sudden action. Then he counted off the shots as they crashed out in the silence. He only had the one rifle, he thought tensely to himself and he couldn't use his hand gun at that range. Six shots, then silence.

Without pausing to think, he scrambled to his feet, thrust himself over the lip of the gully and raced for the knoll. A hundred yards, fifty. Still there was no gunfire from the trees.

Then, out of the corner of his eyes, he saw Venner. The other was crouched down in the tall grass, fumbling frantically for the Colt which had become somehow entangled in his frock coat with all of the crawling through the brush. His breath rasping harshly in his throat, dropping his own rifle as he closed in, he called:

'Don't try it, Venner!'

He saw the other lift his head, eyes wide. Then he rolled back, still tugging at his gun. It came free, sunlight glinting on the blue steel of the barrel. Swiftly, the other lined it up on Joel's chest, as his own gun leapt into his fist. The two shots sounded so close together that there was only the one single echo racing over the rocks. Joel felt the burning touch of the slug along the flesh of his upper arm, almost dropped his own weapon with the shock of it, gritted his teeth, pressed again on the trigger. Through the haze of gunsmoke, he saw Venner falling back, shoulders striking the tree behind him as the bullet slammed into him. He fired once again from six feet away, saw the other's face suddenly slacken, the gun tilting from his nerveless fingers to fall into the grass as he went back.

Whistling up his mount, Joel heaved the other's body over the saddle, climbed up behind and rode back into San Antonio.

Fifteen days later, an early morning sun found Joel Fergus and the Coyotero riding along the trail that led out from the Badlands towards Benson. The town lay sprawled in shadow, sunlight flooding over the hills beyond, creeping swiftly towards the buildings on either side of the main street. The sound of their horses was the only noise that disturbed the stillness as they entered the town after riding over the plank bridge spanning the creek.

Cookie Henders moved out on to the boardwalk, sweeping the dust and litter into the street, glanced up in sudden surprise; then came running forward. His gaze fell on the heavy sacks tied to the marshal's saddle.

'You finally caught up with them critters, Marshal,' he said exultantly.

Joel nodded. 'Ain't a single one of them left alive to hang,' he muttered. He rode on, stopped in front of the jailhouse. He was tired, but strangely relaxed. He was looking forward to a good meal and a sleep between sheets. But first he had something to do. Along both sides of the street, he saw people coming out to stare in their direction. Ellis, the banker, came running along the boardwalk.

'You get them, Marshal?' he called.

'We got them,' Joel answered. He untied the sacks, handed them down. 'I figure it's all there. Better get it back into the vaults just in case anybody else takes a shine to it.'

Staggering under the weight, the other nodded his head emphatically. 'I sure will, Marshal, I sure will.'

Stepping down from the saddle, Joel rubbed a hip, glanced up at the Coyotero. 'Better get something to eat,' he said quietly. 'It's been a long trip for both of us.'

The other nodded, stepped down and made his way along to the diner. Joel watched him go, then pushed his way through the small crowd which had gathered in front of the jail. They parted to let him through, but instead of moving into the office, he turned as if a sudden thought had struck him. Lifting his gaze, he looked along the street, off to the far end of town. He could just make out the slender figure moving out of the telegraph office, moving to the middle of the street, looking in his direction, then holding up her skirts as she began to run.

He quickened his pace, the weariness in him temporarily forgotten.

This Large Print Book, for people
who cannot read normal print,
is published under the auspices of

THE ULVERSCROFT FOUNDATION